Seya

The Woman By The Sea

I0607679

A Novella

By

Divya Tombran

Tepui Roraima Publishing Ltd.

Tepui Roraima Publishing
2850 Lakeshore Blvd West
P. O. Box 80036
Etobicoke, Ontario
Canada
M8V 4A1

Printed in the United States of America

Cover Design by: John Mantha

ISBN: 978-1-7753482-1-4

Dedicated to my husband, Ron Keddy, love of my life.

ACKNOWLEDGEMENT

A special thank you to my husband, Ron, who has supported me once again on my second novel. Thanks for your dedication and for giving me this wonderful opportunity to fulfil my dreams as an author.

I'm grateful to all my family and friends, and all my readers who believe in my work and have supported me throughout my venture.

Thanks to John Mantha, my book cover illustrator, for doing a terrific job in capturing the scene for this title.

CHAPTERS

Chapter One

Seya The Evening Shadow

The meaning of her name Seya is evening shadow, dark as the colour of her Indian skin, and she lived by a remote seaside in Guyana in a rickety shack. The few villagers who accidentally ventured her way claimed that the beautiful sixteen-year-old was struck with madness—some kind of crying sickness—and that she was an outcast. Suresh, a tall and slender dark-skinned Indian fellow of only twenty-one, had recently learned of her and, being an outcast himself, he set out to find her . . .

* * *

The rainstorm had just hit the sea on this dark Sunday evening in Guyana, and Suresh was caught in it as he was walking along the shell-strewn seashore of an east coast village. Mighty waves crashed wildly as the howling wind whipped them about, and seagulls were heard squawking high above in the warm air as *candleflies* darted about the cluster of coconut trees lining the shore.

Suresh had travelled on foot well over a mile from his own home, looking for Seya's shack, and by now he was soaked from his curly shoulder-length black hair down to his sandals. But that did not deter him, neither did the darkness of the night. He persisted on, battling the fierce wind as he trudged through the wet sand, seashells, rocks, and driftwood. Eventually, through squinted eyes, he noticed a faint light in the distance, around the curve of the shore, and he steadfastly gravitated towards it.

As he drew closer, he could make out the old shack on stilts, its ragged greenheart wood walls were being pounded by the rain, and a kerosene oil lamp was dangling from the ceiling of the verandah, its flame flickering in the wind as the waves rolled up on the shore. At the bottom-house of the shack, Suresh noticed a canoe tied to the stilts.

From within the shack an oil lamp burned, creating a mysterious ambience, and through the sheer pink curtain of a side window a shapely shadow of a woman was seen. There was no doubt in Suresh's mind that it was no other than the enigmatic Seya. His first thought was to go and knock on her door, but before he could do so, she emerged on the verandah. In the pool of light from the kerosene oil lamp he could see her clearly, a dark-skinned, petite young woman, delicate looking, and tantalisingly draped in a red sari, with raven hair that reached down to her ankles, whipping about in the wind. He was struck by the dark beauty of her face, a visage fine and child-like, resembling the beauty of a black pearl. He had expected a woman in disarray with the madness she was accused of being, instead, she appeared to be a sad and lonely young woman.

With melancholic eyes, she stared out at the boisterous sea for a moment, then she called out the name, "Mister Gareth." She called the name several times, then as though sensing Suresh's presence, she turned to look sideways in his direction. For a moment, she uttered nothing, then in a soft silvery voice said, "Come, take shelter from the rain."

Suresh climbed the outside stairs of the shack and before he got to the verandah, on which was strung an old cotton hammock, she had disappeared inside. The sheer pink curtain, drawn over the window overlooking the verandah, was flapping in the wind, allowing him glimpses inside the shack. An unpainted and worn room served as a sitting room and kitchen, furnished with a decrepit wooden bench, a mat, a coffee table on which was a large conch shell, and against the back wall was a mud stove, the embers still smouldering from recently being used and, by the scent, Seya had cooked curried fish. The tiny dish sink was empty, the dishes now washed and turned down on a small counter, which meant she already had dinner. A pot was now simmering over the embers of the mud stove, emitting the citrusy scent of lime leaves. The walls of the room were bare, except, for a gold-framed picture of the Hindu god Krishna hanging askew, and in a corner was what appeared to be a shrine with *diyas* or little earthen ghee-soaked lamps, brass idols, and fresh flowers. A small transistor radio was on the coffee table and an Indian love song was now playing above the noise of the churning sea.

Suresh stood on the verandah, dripping wet, wondering where Seya was at the moment. Not before long, she emerged from what appeared to be the entrance of a bedroom, a towel in hand, walking softly on bare feet. She came over to the door of the shack and opened it and handed him the towel.

"Thanks for being so caring—" he began, and before he could converse with her, she quickly turned away and went inside, but not before he caught a glimpse of her eyes in the light of the kerosene oil lamp; they were sea-green, wide and sunken, conspicuous against her dark skin. He found himself wondering what madness possessed this beautiful young woman.

He wiped the rain from his face and dried his arms with the towel and then looked out at the tempestuous sea. The rainstorm was sweeping about wildly across the sea now, the wind whistling in the dark of the night, swaying the kerosene oil lamp hanging from the ceiling of the verandah. There was no telling when the rain would stop, and as he stood there listening to the pitter patter on the zinc roof of the shack and the Indian tune playing on the radio, he vacillated between leaving or taking shelter for a while longer, hoping he would get a chance to talk with Seya. Just as he was debating, she emerged from the shack again. This time she brought him a steaming cup of lime leaves' tea. She did not say a word, but rested the enamel cup on the side table between the two old wooden chairs situated against the wall of the verandah.

"You are so kind to me," Suresh said to her this time, and, again, no response, but her face appeared benign.

She paused there for a moment to check the oil in the lamp, her beautiful arms reaching up gracefully, revealing the seductive shape of her sari bodice which clung to her like a second skin, and to add to her appeal, her long black hair was tossed about by the wind. Suresh could not help but to naturally react with a stir of excitement.

He attempted to converse with her again, saying, "Terrible weather we're having, isn't it?"

Again, she did not respond, but cast him a perfunctory glance with an inscrutable expression, then she lowered her eyes and retreated within the shack in a hurry. At this point, Suresh was beginning to think that his trip here was futile for she was either too shy or inhibited to converse with him.

He took the cup of tea she brought him and began sipping on it, pacing the verandah as he did and catching glimpses within the shack, through the curtain blowing in the window. Seya had apparently turned the radio off and was now sitting in front of the shrine in a lotus position, her red sari wrapped tightly against her finely shaped figure, her long hair falling on the floor like a black sea around her. Incense and diyas were burning, and she chanted a Hindu prayer for a while, almost inaudibly, then there was only the sound of the patter of the rain on the zinc roof.

Suresh thought it best to leave then, and he finished the cup of tea and had just rested the cup on the side table when a piercing cry came from within, calling, "Mister Gareth!" Startled, he looked inside and saw Seya rolling around on the bare floor, holding her stomach and crying, and repeatedly calling out the name 'Mister Gareth'.

Suresh looked on and listened for a while, not knowing what to do, then unable to bear the sounds of her sad cries, he followed his intuition and entered the shack. Seya stood up when she saw him, and now she looked like a wild woman, darting terrified glances at him.

Instinctively, Suresh reached out to embrace her, gently saying, "Come, lay your head on my shoulder."

She shook her head and shrank back as if in fear and took to a corner of the room, crouching on the floor and crying even more madly.

"Who has done this to you?" Suresh asked, sensing her pain. "What happened to you?"

Seya did not answer but continued to cry piteously, her poignant cries evincing the sadness and anguish she was experiencing. Helpless, Suresh watched her, not knowing what to do to console her. He wished he could commiserate with her, assuage her pain, take her in his arms and soothe her, but she would not let him. It was painful for him to stand there and see the dejection in her young eyes.

After what seemed like an hour, which was more like a few minutes, Seya gradually began settling down, her cries slowly diminishing until her demeanour became serene, and she spoke softly, saying, "I'm sorry, I'm so sorry. I'm sorry."

"No need to apologise, Seya."

Wiping her eyes with the back of her hand, she asked, "How do you know my name?"

"That's what the villagers call you," Suresh answered. "And my name is Suresh."

She got up then and began saying, "It will rain all night, Suresh—"

"Then I will leave. But can I see you again, Seya?"

She did not give him an answer, but stood with her head now lowered, twirling a strand of hair around her fingers, and he took her silence as a tacit agreement.

Hesitantly, Suresh backed away and exited the shack and closed the door, and he left for home in the rainstorm that night with Seya on his mind.

The young woman touched his heart and he found himself overtaken by a sadness for her, tears trickling from his own eyes. He mused over her, wondering who she was. For someone so young, she had the sadness and pain of one of many decades. Where did she come from? How did she come to live all by herself by the seaside? Why did she sequester herself from the world? What happened in her life? Why was she an outcast? Why was she crying? What made her so afraid? And who was the man Mister Gareth whose name she had called out? What madness had struck this young woman? He could not decipher her mysteries.

It was passed midnight when Suresh returned home, home to his own sadness and pain in life.

* * *

Suresh's story began on an inauspicious, sweltering Friday afternoon. His father Raheem, a successful jeweller who had lived by the seaside village with his wife Bhanu, was racing to get home from work because Bhanu was sick with pneumonia and he could not reach her by telephone. She normally would wait for him every day on the verandah, with two-year-old Suresh clinging to her skirt, and when he did not see them there that day, a visceral feeling of fear overtook him.

He sped up the car, and, as he drew closer to the house, he scanned the big yard to see if perhaps his wife and child were somewhere under the plentiful fruit trees, like they sometimes did, but there was no sign of them there, nor were they in the hammock at the concrete-paved bottom-house. Hurriedly, he parked the car at the bottom-house and rushed up the front stairs.

"Bhanu!" he called as he tried the door only to find it locked.

No answer.

"Bhanu!"

Still no answer. But now he could hear Suresh crying.

He foraged for the door key in his trousers pocket and found it and unlocked the door and burst into the house.

"Bhanu! Why aren't you answering me? Bhanu!"

Still no answer, but just the distressed cry of Suresh. Raheem followed the sound from where it came and it led him to the master bedroom of the five-bedroom house. And sprawled out on the floor was Bhanu, and Suresh was sitting beside her.

"Wake up, Ma, wake up," the child cried as he shook her with his little hands.

Raheem rushed to his wife's side and felt for her pulse. Nothing. And he let out a loud and mournful cry. "Bhanu, oh my beloved Bhanu! Why, God, why have you taken her away from me? Oh, Bhanu, my sweet Bhanu!"

Suresh was too young to remember what happened. The funeral took place just a day later, and for all his crying, he could not bring his Ma back.

Not too long after the funeral, within a three-month span, a beautiful Indian woman by the name of Manjula, young and fair-skinned with long black hair, captured the bereaved heart of Raheem. And they got married in a hurry, in spite of family and friends telling Raheem that he was rushing into things, that he was not giving himself enough time to grieve for his beloved Bhanu, and that he was bare-faced, shameless with no scruples. But Raheem had fortunately fallen in love again and saw it as God giving him a second chance in life. Suresh also had a second chance of having a mother, and the child instantly took a liking to the affable nature of Manjula. It seemed like it was a good match for all three, for Manjula, besides being likeable, was kind and caring, and she was happy and vibrant, and was a hard-working woman, tending to the house chores as a wife, and caring for little Suresh. In fact, she was overjoyed to have a little boy for her son, and she cuddled the dark-skinned child, and fed and bathed him and doted on him, and always made him sugar-cake. Suresh made her long for children of her own, and within a year, Manjula gave birth to a baby boy, Ranbir, and in the next year, she had a daughter, Zara, and both children took Manjula's fair complexion. Little Suresh adored his baby brother and sister, and the three bonded as biological siblings.

Manjula turned out to be a good choice for a wife and mother, proving to Raheem that he had done the right thing by marrying her. And she had reasons to be happy in life for she had a wonderful husband, a man with whom she fell in love deeply and passionately, who was the only man she had ever known, and she lived in a beautiful home and had three lovely children. There was nothing she was in need of for Raheem catered to her every whim, and she so deserved it.

"I will repay you with many more children," she said to Raheem as he took her out for a car ride along the seaside one day.

"You can start right here," Raheem teased her.

She slapped him on the shoulder and smiled. "Neighbour Bertha is looking after the children and we promised her we will be back soon."

When they arrived back home that afternoon, in the peak heat of the day, Neighbour Bertha, a grey-haired, brown-skinned black woman who was always barefoot and wore a red headtie, was at the bottom-house with the three children, Suresh now five years old, and Ranbir two, and Zara was just a baby, whom Neighbour Bertha was holding on her hip.

"Ma, Ma," Suresh cried and ran up to Manjula and hugged her as soon as she alighted from the car. Then he turned to Raheem, and said, "Neighbour Bertha said there's a peacock in the woods, can you take me to see it, Papa?"

"It's too hot to go out in the woods now, Suresh, maybe some other time I will take you," Raheem said.

Suresh pouted and said, "I want to go now, Papa."

Manjula interrupted, saying, "Not now, Suresh. Some other time. The peacock will still be there."

"But I want to go now!" Suresh cried.

"Your father and I will take you later in the day when it's cool," Manjula said.

"No, not later, I want to go now!"

"Listen to your father, Suresh, he doesn't want to go now."

"Okay, okay," Raheem acquiesced, "I'll take you to see the peacock, but we wouldn't be too long."

Suresh hugged his father and then said, "Thank you, Papa."

"You spoil the child," Manjula said. "He should listen to you. When you say no, it means no."

"I spoil all my children," Raheem said, and jokingly added, "It may be the death of me someday."

"Don't talk like that, Raheem," Manjula said.

"Take Ranbir and Zara upstairs, and Suresh and I will go now."

Neighbour Bertha handed baby Zara to Manjula, and she went her way, across the street where she lived, and Manjula went upstairs with the baby and Ranbir.

About an hour after Raheem and Suresh left, Suresh returned home crying. "Papa is sleeping in the woods, Ma."

"What do you mean by saying Papa is sleeping in the woods?"

"A snake bit Papa and put him to sleep."

"Oh my God!" Manjula began wailing. "Oh my God!" She rushed across the street and called Neighbour Bertha. "Neighbour, please take care of my children for a while, I must go and check on my husband. He's in the woods and a snake has bitten him."

"You shouldn't go alone, my dear. Let my grandsons Neville and Niles accompany you. Neville! Niles!"

The two young, strong black men came rushing down the stairs to help.

Neighbour Bertha went over to Manjula's house and remained behind with the three children, and Manjula and the two young men made their way to the woods. Her worst fears came true, for when Manjula and the men made it to Raheem, he was laying in the woods, dead. Manjula fell to her knees and pulled out her hair and beat her chest in crying. Her whole world was suddenly upended by the terrible tragedy, and darkness came upon her heart, and something inside of her died

11

that day with Raheem, and the once vibrant and happy and kind young woman became a different kind of person.

Suresh was on the verandah when Neville and Niles fetched his father's lifeless body up the stairs, and Manjula cried and cried heartbreakingly. He would then realise that his father was dead. Being that young, he did not fully comprehend death, but he knew it was a bad thing. He had lost both his father and mother in a similarly tragic way, both appeared to be sleeping to him, and he turned to Manjula to console him, but she herself needed comforting, and she pushed him aside.

Raheem was placed in an icebox and was to be buried the following day. Suresh watched in bewilderment as family and friends gathered at the house and were wailing and beating their chests. When they left, in the wee hours of the morning, Neighbour Bertha put Ranbir and Zara to bed. Suresh was in a state of numbness. Everything seemed so surreal to him. Neighbour Bertha tried to comfort him as much as she could, then she left, and he was alone with Manjula.

The icebox containing the corpse of Raheem was in the middle of the semi-dark sitting room, and Manjula was sitting on the bare floor beside it, bent over with her face toward the floor and her long hair scattered about her, and she was weeping. Confused and scared, and not knowing what to do, Suresh stood in a corner and silently watched her, but she did not appear to even notice him, she was so distraught. She cried for the rest of the night, incessantly, and sometime during that time Suresh fell asleep on the floor.

He woke to more cries from his stepmother as she began making preparations for the funeral that day. A tailor came by to take measurements for a suit for Raheem and he made it in very little time, and Manjula bathed Raheem and dressed him, crying all the time. The funeral service took place in the peak heat of the afternoon at the bottom-house, and there was even more wailing. Suresh stood beside the coffin and looked at his father for the last time. Raheem was dressed smartly, his handsome face showing the bluish-black signs of death around his lips and eyes. When it was time to close the coffin, Manjula screamed heart-wrenchingly and held on to Raheem's face, and she kissed him on the cheeks and would not let go. The people around her had to tear her away from the coffin so they could close it to take Raheem away to the grave site.

The three children were then left in the care of Neighbour Bertha, who took them upstairs. Suresh stood by the window and watched as the pall-bearers carried his father's coffin off to the burial ground on the long dusty road. And he cried then for he understood that his Papa was never coming back. But he did not have an inkling as to how his life would then unfold.

Family and friends returned from the burial and gathered at the house to commiserate with Manjula. They stayed with her until the early hours of the morning, and when they left, Neighbour Bertha put Ranbir and Zara to sleep, and she left, leaving Suresh alone with Manjula.

Manjula then got a wild cane and came after Suresh. "You're the reason my husband is dead!" she screamed. "If you hadn't insisted on him taking you to the woods the snake would not have bitten him and he would still be alive! Wicked, wicked boy!" And Manjula beat

Suresh that night with the wild cane, leaving him with welts all over his little body.

Immediately after, she regretted her actions and took the boy and sponge-bathed him, and she oiled his skin with coconut oil with tenderness. She dressed him in his pyjamas and lifted him in her arms and lulled him to sleep, then she placed him in her bed and covered him with a blanket and she went to sleep beside him. The next morning when she woke up, a bout of pain and grief struck her again, and she began blaming the child again for the death of her husband.

And so began a different kind of life for Suresh. One moment Manjula would despise him, and after she vented her anger, she would become remorseful. On the occasions when she was angry at him, she would go around telling everyone that Suresh had killed his father, that he was born on an inauspicious day and that he was a cursed child. Soon Suresh became stigmatised and was ostracised by her and her family and friends, and was deemed an outcast. Suresh was susceptible at that tender age and he believed that he had killed his father, and that was a heavy burden of guilt he had to live with for a child so young.

Manjula was set for life with the wealth Raheem had left her from his jewellery business, and she had the house that was equipped with modern amenities, having electricity, a dial-up telephone, even a gas stove, and she was also left with the car in her possession. But nothing could appease Manjula, nor could she be comforted or consoled by her family and friends. She not only blamed Suresh, but she also directed her anger at God, cursing Him repeatedly for causing such a terrible tragedy to happen to her at her young age.

Sincerely believing that Suresh was a cursed child for he had caused the death of Raheem, she decided she would punish him, and instead of sending the child to school, she sent him to work at a local carpenter's shop at the tender age of five, and she took almost all of his paltry income. When her children, Ranbir and Zara, became of age she sent them to school, and when the children asked why Suresh was working instead of going to school, she told the children that Suresh had killed their father, that he was dark and evil and that they were fair and good.

As children, Ranbir and Zara did not take her too seriously, but when they became youngsters in their teens, they started to question their mother. Manjula's cantankerous behaviour became more and more erratic, and she turned on her own children for not believing her. Unlike her children, who were too young to remember Raheem when he died, Suresh understood her situation because he too was grieving the loss of his father, and being conditioned that he was at fault, he wanted to do whatever he could to console his stepmother. In fact, he would feel sorry for her in spite of her love-hate relationship with him, because, right after getting angry at him, she would become remorseful and his tender heart would forgive her.

Ranbir and Zara grew to despise their mother for she often threw fits of temper tantrums at them. Things became so unbearable for them that when they became of age they applied to study abroad, and they left their mother behind and did not look back. Manjula then clung to Suresh, becoming more and more controlling, and possessive of him. Things then got so intolerable for Suresh that he built himself a shed on Manjula's property and he moved out of the house. But that did not stop Manjula from manipulating him and playing on his tender side, keeping him chained to her with the guilt that he had killed his father.

Now at a marriageable age, Suresh wanted to take a wife, but Manjula hindered his attempts by bad-mouthing him in an effort to keep him imprisoned in her demented world, she so badly needed someone to cling to. Suresh was left trapped in a world of ennui and despair, trapped in the miserable dark abyss of Manjula, with no escape in sight.

* * *

Coming home after his encounter with Seya was something Suresh did not want to reveal to Manjula for he knew she would become incensed if he did. As he came in sight of her house, situated a short way inland from the seashore, he noticed the verandah lights were on. When he drew closer, he saw that Manjula was sitting on a chair on the wrap-around verandah—a slight and attractive woman, dressed in a voluptuous silk green evening robe—peering through the rain at Suresh as he unlatched the gate and entered the yard. Suresh knew she would admonish him for something as innocuous as coming home late, so he braced himself.

Manjula hurried down the stairs to confront him. "Where have you been so late in the night?"

"I was out for a walk," Suresh answered.

"A walk in the rain?" she asked skeptically.

"Yes, Ma," Suresh said, for that was all she needed to know.

"Don't let it happen again!" she shouted at him. Suresh expected an apology to ensue after her outburst, he knew Manjula that well, and, sure enough, almost

16

immediately, she said, "Sorry, child, I didn't mean to shout at you."

Manjula always had a look about her when she was sorry that was bona fide and pitiful, and, like he had done countless times before, Suresh forgave her, and went on to ask, "Have you had dinner this evening, Ma."

"No, I've been too down and depressed to do so," Manjula said. "I haven't eaten a morsel since midday."

"Then let me prepare you something to eat," he offered.

"That wouldn't be necessary," Manjula said.

"I can't let you go to bed hungry, Ma."

"Nonsense!"

"Then goodnight, Ma," Suresh said, and as Manjula turned to make her way back up the stairs, he went straight to his shed which was situated right behind the house.

There he was greeted by his faithful friend, a black and tan German Shepherd named Rex. The dog was waiting for him at the entrance and stood up on his hind legs to paw him, wagging his tail as he did and panting with his tongue hanging out. This immediately brought a smile to Suresh's face, and he bent down and gave him a good rubbing on his coat, saying, "Come, my old friend, let's go for a walk in the yard."

Rex barked in agreement, and Suresh took him for a walk in the big yard that was scattered with fruit trees, of mostly mangoes, guavas and coconuts, the fragrances mingling, enhanced by the earthy smell of the rain and warmth of the midnight. At this late hour, the neighbours had turned into bed, their lights extinguished, and the only sounds were those of the rain falling and the chirring of crickets. Given his affinity with nature and animals, Suresh enjoyed this peaceful and quiet time alone with his dog. It played a great part in surviving the miserable conditions of his life. And, tonight, he stayed out later than usual, relishing the moments.

It was still raining incessantly when he and the dog returned to the old wooden shed, and Suresh lit the kerosene oil lamp hanging from the ceiling. The shed had no electricity and the atmosphere was stiflingly hot as usual. The small space was immaculately kept, and sparsely furnished, with a ragged wooden armchair, a small kitchen table and two chairs, a cot over which draped a mosquito netting, a hammock strung in the middle of the room, and a clothes-horse in a corner, on which hung the few pieces of clothing Suresh possessed. There were two small windows, which Suresh left shut tonight to keep out the rain. The wooden floor was bare and swept clean, and against the back wall of the shed protruded a mud stove and dish sink. At one corner of the cot was a night table where Suresh kept his only source of entertainment; a mouth organ. Right beside the shed was a cubicle for a bathroom, and a latrine was further down in the backyard.

As soon as Suresh lit the lamp, he got a rag and dried Rex's coat and he left him sitting on the bare floor and went outside to have a bath. Before heading to the cubicle, he noticed that all the lights in Manjula's house were off, which was an indication that she had obviously gone to sleep, either that or she had passed out from fatigue and hunger. Suresh put her in the back of his mind for now, and he bathed and got dressed in his pyjama trousers only. He then got his mouth organ and ensconced himself comfortably in the hammock, with Rex sitting at his feet. Rex had a penchant for Indian music, and it was Suresh's habit to serenade him in the nights, and bring some equanimity to himself, and he began playing an Indian love tune as he slapped off the mosquitoes that were biting into his arms and legs from time to time.

It did not take Rex very long to begin snoring. Becoming somnolent himself, and having to go to work the following day, Suresh put the mouth organ away and went and lit a mosquito coil and placed it in a corner of the cot. He then extinguished the oil lamp and settled on the cot beneath the mosquito netting. Rex woke up and went and laid on the floor by the head side of the cot, where he usually slept in the nights.

It was pitch black in the shed now, except, for the glowing red tip of the mosquito coil. As Suresh listened to the buzzing of the mosquitos against the netting, he watched as the incense-scented smoke curled and drifted about, and he could hear the chirring of the crickets outside.

Seya came to his mind in the darkness, like an evening shadow, as was the meaning of her name. He tried to assimilate his encounter with her. She was not mad as the villagers assumed, he thought, but he surmised that she was stricken with a heartbreak that resulted in a crying sickness. Who broke the young heart of Seya? Was it the man Mister Gareth? What really happened to her? Suresh could not help but being drawn to her dark, ethereal beauty, and something else. He had made the comparison of their lives. They were both ostracised, both outcasts of society. That was what they had in common. That was why he ventured out to make contact with her in the first place. Could she have sensed that in him, also? Was that why she invited him in to take shelter from the rain? There was never a word that she had done so for any of the villagers. And she brought him a towel to dry himself and had served him tea and made him feel special. He knew very little in the way of benevolence of others, much of which he remembered of his father but not his mother, as he was too young when she had passed away, and before his father had died Manjula had shown him much kindness and love. The only other person who was kind to him was Neighbour Bertha.

With only that one encounter with her, Seya, the dark angel had touched that secret place in his heart and brought alive feelings he had never had for any other woman; romantic feelings that he knew only through Indian love movies, of lovers running through fields of flowers or dancing in the rain and singing deeply passionate songs. He laid there dreaming of running his fingers through her long black hair, and letting her rest her head on his shoulders and cry—cry until her sea-green eyes had no tears left, cry until the salt of her tears mended and healed her wounded heart, cry until her tears became tears of happiness.

As Suresh drifted off to sleep, he said to himself, "I just have to see her again, and I must find out what really happened to Seya."

Chapter Two

Suresh The Carpenter

It rained overnight and was still raining at the crowing of the *fowlcocks* in the seaside village. Rex stirred at precisely 4 o'clock, like he normally did, and he remained on the floor for a moment longer, savouring the last moments of sleep in the darkness. Once the dog was fully awake, he got under the mosquito netting to find Suresh was still fast asleep, snoring heavily. Gently, he pawed at his master's chest. Suresh turned aside and laid there, not wanting to get out of bed. He dreaded going to work, not because of the work itself, as he took pride in his work in carpentry, but because of his horrible boss. Suresh felt like not wanting to work today, but Rex kept on pawing him, as was the usual act in the mornings, until he became fully awake and realised that not going to work was not an option.

"Good morning, my friend," he said to the dog as he patted him affectionately on the head. Rex barked in response then licked Suresh's hand before Suresh rolled out of his cot. Straightaway, he fumbled about in the dark and went over to the kitchen table and groped about to find the matches, and he lit the kerosene oil lamp hanging from the ceiling. Today was a work day and he had to cook breakfast and lunch and get ready to leave.

As was his habit, he would first bathe, and he grabbed a towel and his toothbrush and headed out the door. Immediately, he noticed that Manjula's car, which was usually parked at the bottom-house, was gone, which he found odd. He wondered what she was up to this early in the morning but did not spend much time on it; she was always up to no good, which he did not care to know about. He dismissed the thought and proceeded to the cubicle and had a bath.

When he returned to the shed, he got dressed then lit the mud stove and went about making *dosea* and fried eggs for breakfast. He then put a pot of lime leaves' tea to boil and sat back on the old armchair and waited for it to draw. He watched as the smoke curled its way up from the mud stove and mingled with the delicious smell of the dosea and fried eggs and citrusy scent of the lime leaves, and Seya came to his mind. There was a sadness about her that clawed at him and he wanted to see her again that evening, but he knew if he did Manjula might get suspicious and find out about her, something he wanted to avoid, to protect Seya. He picked up his mouth organ and played an Indian tune and serenaded Rex for a while, and when the tea was finished drawing, he sat at the kitchen table and ate breakfast and fed Rex a hearty portion of it.

By now, the neighbours were up; you could tell by the sound of the chopping of wood and the clanging of pots and pans, and voices chattering. The animals were up, also, mooing and braying and barking, and meowing. And a baby girl was heard crying, like she always did at this early hour of the morning, wanting to be breastfed by her mother.

By the time Suresh and Rex finished breakfast, the cries of the baby girl subsided, and Suresh went on to cook some rice and *aloo* curry for lunch, and he packed the hot food in a flask. He worked like a mule all day and it was good to have a hot lunch, which he always looked forward to.

Leaving his dog behind, though, was something he never looked forward to. He patted Rex on the head and said, "It's time for me to go to work, my friend. Be a good boy till I get back." Rex gave a small whine and reluctantly followed Suresh to the door. He was always unhappy to see his master go and, sometimes, would pull some kind of trick for him to stay.

Suresh was looking for his sandals but found only one. "Where's my other sandal, Rex?" he asked the dog.

Rex had hidden it.

"Come on, boy, get me my sandal so I can go to work."

Rex gave him a sorry look and just sat down.

Suresh always kept bone treats in the event of such a thing happening, and he went and got one. "Go get my sandal and I'll give you a treat," he said to the dog.

Rex sat there for a while longer, looking at him as though he did not understand.

Suresh tugged at the dog's ear, and repeated, "Now, boy, go get my sandal and I'll give you a treat."

Rex then went and fetched the sandal, which he had hidden under the clothes-horse, and he brought it to Suresh, dropping it at his feet, and Suresh in turn gave him the treat. "Now, don't you pull this trick on me again, okay, pal, or I'd be late for work," Suresh said as he buckled on the sandals. "I wish I could stay with you all day, but I have to go to work now."

Rex took the treat but made a sad and sorry face. Suresh ruffled his coat affectionately then let him outside, where he sat in the shelter, beneath the extended corrugated zinc roof of the shed, and ate his treat. There he would anxiously wait for Suresh to return home.

The downpour was even heavier now, beating hard against the greenheart walls of the shed. Suresh cloaked himself in a raincoat and headed off on his bicycle to work, with his lunch flask dangling from the handlebar. The carpentry shop was a few miles away, and instead of taking the usual route which was unpaved and filled with too many potholes and puddles, he made a detour through the seaside village, which was now stirring with early morning activities. Kerosene oil lamps were burning in the little old houses on stilts where people were preparing breakfast, spicy aromas escaping the pots on mud stoves and mingling with the smoke from the wood, while those who lived more of a modern existence with electricity, had their gas stoves burning. Some were dabbing their earthen bottom-houses with a mixture of cowdung and clay, while the ones with concrete were being swept with *pinta brooms*. A few men from the village were on their way to work at this time, rice field workers and sugarcane cutters, cloaked in raincoats and were barefooted, carrying cutlasses in their hands as they trudged through the dirt streets. Ladies, some in worn frocks and others in saris, were on their way to the market to sell baskets of fishes and vegetables, some on foot steadying the baskets on their heads, and others on donkey-carts. A few cyclists manoeuvred their way through the streets, passing donkeys and cows, and chickens pecking at the street side grass. The occasional cars tooted their horns as they drove along the dirt road, with one of them getting stuck in a pothole and making a racket in trying to spin out of it. The air was warm and the smell of the place was of fresh earth with the rain falling, mingled with the salty breeze coming in from the sea. Suresh just loved the mysterious ambiance of a rainy morning in the seaside village.

He whistled a tune as he passed houses where children were playing in barrels of water in the rain, splashing the water about and giggling, then he came to a strip of small businesses along the way, some shops now opened while others were still closed at this time. As he passed the small market, which was just an open space, people were setting up stalls covered with plastic to keep out the rain, and they displayed their fresh fruits and vegetables on small stands. A fisherman had just come in from the sea and was haggling with vendors over the fresh fishes, piled in the back of a truck. After passing through this acrid, fishy-smelling part of the village, Suresh rode a short way until he came to the carpentry shop, a small, old wooden building painted dark blue. Immediately, he noticed Manjula's car was parked up front. He hurriedly parked his bicycle, and just as he turned to approach her, she pulled away.

He stood there staring after her, and as he was wondering why she would come this early to the shop, his boss, Abdul, who was obviously in cahoots with Manjula, met him at the door entrance and hollered at him, saying, "You're five minutes late for work!"

Suresh wanted to tell him he was delayed because Rex had hidden his sandal, but Abdul would only think he was making up an alibi, so he did not bother to give a reason.

Abdul was a slave driver, mean and nasty. He was a heavy-set Indian man in his mid-forties, with a paunch and a head of thin hair that had already turned grey. He was single, and the only female friend he kept was Manjula. He was beguiled by Manjula's fair beauty and would do just about anything for her. Manjula used him to furnish her home with ornate furniture that he built personally, and she got him to run errands whenever she needed him. Like she had done with the other villagers, Manjula poisoned his mind against Suresh since he was a little boy when she had sent him to work for Abdul at the age of five, telling Abdul that Suresh had killed his father. And Abdul believed her story and mistreated Suresh to punish him for his bad deed, working him like a donkey and paying him way less than he deserved. Suresh did not know any better and could not do better, and he kept on working for him. That was the only life Suresh knew and he did not know how to break out of the cycle of mistreatments from both Abdul and Manjula. So, with gritted teeth, he took the abuse. There was no one else he could turn to, for Manjula made sure Suresh stayed an outcast by telling everyone that Suresh had killed his father, and Suresh was ostracised by all with whom he came in contact, except, for Neighbour Bertha who refused to believe a bad word Manjula would tell her about Suresh, in fact, she was always quick to defend Suresh.

As Suresh entered the gloomy shop, stuffy with sawdust and smelling of varnish, Abdul shouted at him belligerently, saying, "I will deduct half an hour of your pay for being late! Go to work right away so you don't waste any more time. I want a cabinet done by the end of the day for a customer. And if you don't complete it, I will deduct more of your wages! You're nothing but a good-for-nothing!"

Abdul made Suresh's blood boil, but there was nothing he could do about it. He could not yell back at him for that would only make matters worse, for he had tried doing so on an occasion, and had sucked his teeth at Abdul and Abdul had boxed his ears. And Suresh could not defy him and fight back, because he would end up losing his job. He was caught in a catch-22 situation. So he suffered silently, saying not a word out of fear and intimidation, wondering how long he would be able to sustain the abuse.

With anger still searing, he got down to working on the sitting room cabinet he was instructed to finish by the end of the day. He picked out fine pieces of hububalli wood which he precisely measured and commenced sawing. "*You're nothing but a good-for-nothing,*" he could hear Abdul's words ringing in his mind, and as those words reverberated, he clutched the saw tighter, sawing vigorously, his hands trembling as he did. "*You're doomed,*" a voice inside his head said, "*you're trapped in a miserable life with no way out!*" The veins in his hands were now swelling as though they would explode with rage, and he kept on sawing, arduously, faster and faster, trying to saw away his hurt and anger. "*You killed your father,*" he could now hear Manjula saying. Sweat was now pouring down his handsome dark face, and his shoulder-length, curly black hair became damp, the strands clinging to his neck. As Manjula's voice kept echoing in his ears, he sawed even harder and harder and was now sweating until his shirt and trousers became soaked, then there was a sudden relief.

He moved on to the other phase of the cabinet, putting the pieces together, and thinking someday he will glue his life together. And as he moved on to sanding the furniture, he felt a calm come over him, as he thought that someday he will smooth things in his life. The last phase was varnishing, and he took his time in dreaming of polishing his life until it would shine someday.

That was how Suresh made it through his work days with Abdul, by sweating out his anger and dreaming that someday things would change, that there would be a cessation of his troubles, for he convinced himself that nothing lasts forever.

He was given no breaks in the mornings and afternoons, and only fifteen minutes for lunch. By lunch time, he had regained his composure. He got his flask of hot food, and sat down on a bench and began eating.

Abdul came strolling over to where he was, and by the sneer on his face Suresh knew he had nothing good to say to him.

Mockingly, he said, "I heard you were with Myra last night," Myra being a prostitute of the village.

Suresh felt his anger rising again, and flabbergasted by the preposterous news, he asked, "You heard what?"

"Don't tell me you've forgotten her name already," Abdul said contemptuously as he laughed.

Suresh wanted to clarify things but he refrained from doing so because he did not want to mention Seya, to protect her. "Who told you so?" he asked, knowing that it had to be no other than Manjula, whom he had seen leaving when he arrived at work that morning.

"The whole village will know by the end of the day, Manjula will make sure they do," Abdul said. "You dirty scoundrel! You and Myra deserve each other," Abdul went on to say.

Manjula had obviously surmised that he had been with Myra last night when he went home late, and she believed her assumption. Another slander from her, he thought, only this time it did not involve his father. He left his lunch unfinished and gritted his teeth as he resumed work, working off his anger and frustrations all over again.

He completed the cabinet with expert craftsmanship and inspected it keenly before he began hand-brushing it with another coat of varnish. It was the end of his work day by the time he was finished with the task, then he went to collect his pay from Abdul, which he paid daily in cash. The sum was short half an hour, as he expected, from his already paltry income, but there was no point of making a fuss, for Manjula took most of his wages, anyway, and, furthermore, he could not bear another upset for the day, so he took the money without saying anything and left for the local market while the rain had just eased.

A fresh catch of catfish had just arrived at the market when Suresh got there, so was fresh beef brought in by the butcher, and after deliberating for a moment, he decided to select a fat, live catfish to curry for dinner, along with a parcel of fresh shrimps to cook with some *chorai callaloo*, which he would pick from Manjula's garden.

He then meandered his way through the market on his bicycle, taking in the scent of the fresh fishes and fruits and vegetables, and the earthy smell from the rain. And as he stopped at a stall to inspect a crisp parcel of Scotch Bonnet hot peppers, he noticed her there, the prostitute Myra, endowed with sheer beauty, dressed in a short tiger-patterned frock and wearing high-heeled red slippers, her jet-black hair hanging loose down to her waist, her fair face made up with pink rouge and red lipstick. And she smelled wonderfully heavenly of gardenia perfume.

She coquettishly sought out his eyes and smiled at him, but not before three ladies, friends of Manjula selling at the market, caught her in her act.

"Manjula was right, Suresh is seeing that 'bad woman'," one of them whispered.

"I just saw her smiling at him," another one said.

"I saw it too," said the other.

Suresh noticed them and immediately could tell what they were talking about—his supposed rendezvous with Myra that Manjula had obviously told them about—so he averted his face away from Myra and bought the parcel of Scotch Bonnet hot peppers, and he continued along. The women gave him the cold shoulder as he passed by, but Suresh had grown so use to this kind of treatment that he ignored them, though he winced inwardly.

A woman of no scruples, Myra never purported to be anything else but herself. Having no compunction of ignominy, and not inhibited in any way, she was out hustling this late afternoon. She had noticed Suresh several times before but had always thought he was too poor to afford her services, but today she noticed the cash in his wallet when he was paying for the hot peppers, so she targeted him and was tailing his every move. She caught up with him as he was leaving the market, and she deliberately walked ahead, flaunting herself in her red high-heeled slippers. Turning back, she pretended she was surprised to see him again and, looking askance at him, said, "Are you following me, lover boy?"

"It seems the other way around, lovers' girl," Suresh responded as he pedalled his bicycle alongside of her.

"Rumours have it that you have no friends and that you are a very lonely young man," she said rather audaciously. "It's such a shame that a good-looking fellow like you should be alone." She walked slightly ahead of him now, *whining* her hips as she did, and trying to tease him with her swaying legs. Then she threw her head over her shoulder flirtatiously and said, "I can be your friend if you'd like. Meet me at Freddy's house up the street and I'll keep your company tonight."

Suresh brought his bicycle to a stop, and she halted her steps, misconstruing that she had gotten him interested. And he asked, "Why, Myra, why?"

"Why what? I thought you were going to ask how much," she said, giving him an askew smile.

"Why do you do what you do, gal? You've come from a well-to-do family whom you're only disgracing, as well as yourself. Why waste your life when you could have settled down with someone decent and have a respectable life?"

"It's a long story," Myra said as she seductively brushed her hair back with her long, manicured fingernails. "But if you have the time, come now and see me and I'll tell you all about it. How much money do you have on you? I take only cash, no trust or credit."

On a rainy, sultry day like that day, others would have been inebriated with desire for her, stupefied by the mere suggestion and succumb to her, but Suresh was not that susceptible, for all her beauty, Myra could not stir him, in fact, he rejected her amorous advances and pitied her. "No thank you, Myra. I don't need your service," he said to her dismissively.

"What is wrong with me? Or, do you have someone else in your life?" she asked, rather disappointedly, and in a last effort to attract him, she stuck out her plunging décolletage at him.

"Go home and think about what I've told you, Myra," Suresh said with great solemnity.

Reluctantly, Myra turned to leave, and, sadly, Suresh watched as she walked down the street to Freddy's little brothel.

Manjula's friends at the market had been watching this exchange from a distance, and one of them said, "He's making plans to meet with her again. Dirty boy!"

"Dirty, dirty, boy!" the other two friends exclaimed.

When Myra turned into Freddy's house, Suresh rode off and headed home.

* * *

"You're short on your pay," Manjula said when he handed her the larger part of his wages at the bottom of the front stairs, where she waited for him every work day.

"I was late by five minutes this morning and Abdul deducted half an hour," Suresh explained.

"Get up earlier in the mornings so you don't have to be late for work!" Manjula shouted as she tucked the bank notes in her brassiere.

"Rex had hidden—" Suresh began, then changed his mind about explaining the situation to Manjula. Whatever he said would be ridiculed harshly. As he looked at her, he noticed how pale and sickly she looked and in that moment he felt pity for her, then a bout of hurt suddenly crept up within him as he thought of how she had spread false rumours about him and Myra to Abdul and the ladies at the market.

He watched as she turned and began heading back up the stairs, and he thought of broaching the subject of Myra, but decided against it, for he would rather put his reputation on the line and let her believe that he was with Myra, rather than taking the risk of having her find out about Seya. Besides, if he were to confront her with slandering him, she would first vehemently deny it, then she would admit it and become apologetic and shed crocodile tears to make him feel sorry for her, so it was best to leave things alone for the sake of Seya.

"Goodnight," he bid her as she continued up the stairs.

She did not reply but went inside and slammed the door shut.

Suresh then turned and headed for the shed.

The deluge of rain had resumed, and he found Rex where he had left him, sheltering under the zinc roof of the shed. When the dog saw him, he greeted him with a wagging tail, and that immediately took away the hurt he was feeling, replaced by a joy that only the dog could bring him. He bent down and ruffled the dog's coat and patted him on the head, then after taking him inside and giving him a bone treat, he went about cleaning the catfish and shrimps in the dish sink. He then went in the garden and picked some chorai callaloo and returned to the shed and cleaned those, also.

As he was now sitting on the *peerah* on the bare floor grinding curry spices on the masala brick for the catfish curry, there was a knock on the door, and he looked up to find Neighbour Bertha with an umbrella in one hand and a baking pan in the other. She was now in her mid-seventies, and still going barefoot, an agile black woman dressed in an immaculate white cotton frock with a red headtie that accentuated her deep brown skin that was smooth and taut for her age, and her black eyes were deep and sunken.

"May I come in?" she asked. "I've brought you a pan of *cassava pone*."

Suresh got up and said, "Come in, come in. I'm just preparing dinner." And he took her umbrella, and the cassava pone, and said, "My favourite cake. Thank you. I'll have it after dinner."

After rinsing her feet with a bucket of water which was just outside the shed, Neighbour Bertha entered the shed and towel-dried her feet, then she asked, "What's for dinner?"

"Catfish curry and callaloo with shrimp, and rice."

"Let me help you with cleaning the rice," she offered.

"Okay. Would you be staying for dinner?" Suresh asked before measuring the rice.

"No, honey, I've just had an early dinner."

Suresh measured a cup of rice and placed it in a bowl, and Neighbour Bertha gathered her frock and took a seat on a peerah and began picking the soiled grains of rice and putting them aside in a bowl. Suresh then placed some wood in the mud stove and lit it, and he put on a pot of water to boil for the rice.

Puckering her grey, thinning eyebrows, Neighbour Bertha asked, "Eh, eh, what is this I heard that you were with Myra last night?"

"You heard so too," Suresh said without flinching with surprise.

"Manjula told me herself, and I don't believe a word! Neither do I believe that you killed your father. I was a midwife for years, and I helped to deliver you, and you were a healthy and good baby, not cursed like Manjula would have people believe. Your mother Bhanu was a good and decent woman and there's no way she would have given birth to an evil child." After pausing for a moment, she went on to say, "I know how you must be feeling over this, because people are saying bad things about me, too."

"Like what?"

"I was coming home from the market one day, and as I was passing the elementary school a group of children started running away from me, saying that I am a *fire-rass*! And they spread it around the school and to their parents. Now everyone in this small village thinks I'm a fire-rass. And, furthermore, the rumours have it that I deal in *obeah*. I'll tell you, boy, I've never sucked blood and I've never meddled in witchcraft or black magic."

"I've known you since I was a baby, Neighbour Bertha, and I know you're a good, God-fearing woman."

"Now, even Manjula believes the rumours. In fact, she's scared of me. She thinks I will enter the keyhole of her door one night and suck her blood dry."

"That may be a good thing that she's scared of you," said Suresh and smiled. "That way she can't take her eyes and pass you. Being scared means she wouldn't take advantage of you or show you any disrespect."

Neighbour Bertha then got up and washed the rice in the dish sink and put it on to boil, and she returned to the peerah and was watching Suresh as he resumed grinding the curry spices on the masala brick. "I wish you would find a nice wife to grind your masala for you, boy," she said.

"A wife? How am I going to find a wife when all the women in the village think I killed my father?"

"There must be one who would not believe this nancy story."

Suresh's mind then ran on Seya. He wondered if she would believe the story. Maybe it would not matter to her one way or the other, because she was in love with Mister Gareth and maybe she would be this mysterious man's wife someday. He chose not to mention her to Neighbour Bertha at that moment.

"You must find a wife for yourself, boy. Or one will fall from heaven one day. She will know how to cook and clean and bear you many children. This is not the kind of life for a young man. You're of marriageable age and now is the time to start a new life."

"I don't know what Manjula would do without me around. She bad-mouths me then turns around and feels sorry so she can keep me around, for she knows I am the only one who understands what she's going through, and I'm the only one who cares about what she's going through, for we both go through the same grief and pain over my father's death."

"She will survive without you, Suresh. She will always have Abdul to lean on."

"She wouldn't let go of me that easily."

"Her own children, Ranbir and Zara, left her because of her disposition, and you can't stick around and be the object of her bad-mouthing for the rest of your life."

"Believe me, Neighbour Bertha, I want to marry and start a new life, but that would have to be far away from here, not in this village."

"If you must leave this village to go to another to find a wife, then do so. You're young and have good experience in carpentry and with that you can start life anywhere."

The rice began bubbling now, and Suresh rose and began cooking the chorai callaloo with shrimps, then he threw on the catfish and began currying it.

Neighbour Bertha then said. "I'm going to visit my daughter in the west coast."

"How long will you be gone for?"

"I'll be gone for a few weeks. I need to get away from these bad rumours and relax my old head for a while."

"Would Neville and Niles be going also?"

"No, my grandsons have to attend to the garden and make a living," Neighbour Bertha answered, then lapsed into silence for a moment as she thought of the two orphan children, for both her son, their father, and daughter-in-law were killed in a car accident when they were just boys and they were left in her care, and now they were the ones caring for her in her old age as she was now a widow.

"Sure you don't want to stay for dinner?" Suresh asked.

"Thanks for the offer, honey, but I must go and pack my things to leave tomorrow. I'll see you when I get back." And with that, Neighbour Bertha left.

As the fish curry was boiling, giving off appetising whiffs, Suresh looked out the front door of the shed at Manjula's kitchen. No smoke was coming from the window, which meant she was too sick to cook and feed herself. She was probably lying around in bed now, languishing away in her grief and pain and misery. Suresh's tender heart could not help but feeling bad for her. Any time he saw her in that state he too would feel grief and pain, for she was there to constantly remind him of his father's death. If his father were alive, she would have been a different woman, a happy one, like she used to be before his death. She would have replaced the loving mother he had lost. How he wished for that, for Manjula, beautiful Manjula, to be a mother to him once again. That's all he wanted from her. And he was willing to tolerate her behaviour so long as there was hope that she would come to her senses one day and be the woman she once used to be when she used to bathe him and oil his skin and cuddle him, and shower him with kisses. And anytime she would apologise to him for her bad behaviour, he would entertain a glimmer of hope and clutch on to it.

When the catfish curry and chorai callaloo were finished cooking, he dished out a steaming plate with rice, and he got a mango which he had picked earlier in the orchard, and he headed over to Manjula's house.

When he opened the front door, the place was in darkness, so he switched on the light and called, "Ma!"

No answer.

"Ma!" he called again.

A weak voice from within her bedroom asked, "What do you want?"

"I've brought you some dinner."

"I'm not hungry."

"Have you eaten anything today?"

"Not since breakfast," Manjula said.

"So you haven't had lunch and it's time you get out of bed and have something to eat for dinner."

"Your father is dead, Suresh."

"And you'll die, too, if you don't look after yourself," Suresh said.

Manjula came out of the bedroom and stood in the hallway, and even though her hair was dishevelled and she looked pale and sickly, she still looked as beautiful as he remembered her as a child when she used to play with him.

Suresh wanted to hug her but refrained because she would only push him away, instead, he said, "You can't bring back Pa, neither can I, Ma. Don't waste away grieving over him. Here, have something to eat for dinner." And Suresh led her to the kitchen table and sat her down.

"Sometimes I wonder how you could care about someone like me," Manjula said, thinking how she had bad-mouthed him with Abdul and the ladies at the market just that morning.

"Because I don't know how to be mean and nasty," Suresh responded. "It's simply not my nature."

With that, Suresh left her and returned to the shed, and he sat down to a scrumptious dinner with Rex and they ate to their hearts' replete. After dinner, he tidied up the place, had a bath, then ensconced himself in the hammock and played a tune on the mouth organ for Rex, both enjoying the solace that it brought.

His mind then wandered to Seya. He wondered what she was doing at the moment, if she was crying and calling out Mister Gareth's name. He could not help but thinking they were two very sad and lonely people in the world. That night when he laid his head on his pillow, he cried, releasing his anguish and frustrations before falling to a sound sleep.

Chapter Three

Ostracising Seya

The following morning Suresh woke before Rex did, which was not the usual case. He had closed the windows of the shed the night before due to the rainfall and the stifling heat of the place was literally burning up his body. He peered through the mosquito netting and found Rex was snoring on the bare floor. Careful not to wake the dog, he lifted the mosquito netting and tip-toed over to the window beside the bed and shoved it open. The rain had stopped, replaced by a clear moonlit sky, and a beam of moonlight poured into the warm room with the gust of a pleasant breeze. Quietly, Suresh returned to the cot and lay there a moment longer under the netting, listening to the chirping sound of the crickets coming from the orchard, and staring at the crescent moon.

Seya dawned on his mind then. He imagined her sleeping in her shack by the seashore, all alone, as he was. He fantasised of laying close to her and taking her in his arms and loving her, loving all the hurt out of her, and his fantasy strayed to things he had never done before, of holding her hands and kissing her and making love to her.

He was deep into his pleasurable thoughts when a candlefly flew into the room, interrupting his reverie with its blinking yellow light, and he traced its movement as it buzzed about Rex's ears and woke the dog. Right away, Rex got under the netting and began pawing Suresh on his chest.

"I've been up long before you, old boy," Suresh said to the dog and rubbed his head affectionately. And he rolled out of the cot and began his morning with lighting the kerosene oil lamp hanging from the ceiling.

This morning he felt like having a hot coco tea before his bath, so he got some wood and lit the mud stove and put on a pot of water to boil, and he went outside to brush his teeth. Manjula's car, he noticed, was parked at the bottom-house, which meant she was not off making trouble this early morning. The rain the day before had made the path to the cubicle muddy, so he walked on the dewy grass and got to the cubicle and turned on the pipe and brushed his teeth.

By the time he returned to the shed the water was boiling, and he made himself a cup of coco with evaporated milk, and he sat down on the old armchair relishing every sip, and taking in the peaceful ambiance of the morning as he watched the flame of the lamp wavering, which attracted a moth that was banging up against the glass of the lamp. He loved this time of the morning the most when all the neighbours were still asleep, as were the sources of his pain in life; Manjula and Abdul. The crackling of the wood in the mud stove was the only sound, and he found that soothing, along with the aromatic wisps of smoke that drifted about in the warm shed. This equanimity was a pleasant respite from his dreadful days. And it was also comforting to have his best friend sit by his side, on the bare floor, keeping his company. By now, he thought, he might have gone insane if it was not for Rex keeping his mind sound.

He savoured his coco tea for as long as he could, made another cup, then he had his bath and made breakfast, which he had with Rex, after which, he prepared his lunch for work. This morning Rex did not pull any trick on him, so he left on time.

Although it was a bright and sunny morning, his usual route to work was muddy with the rainfall the day before, so he took the route through the market again. The market was already bustling, and Manjula's three friends gave him a dirty look when he passed by them, thinking that he had been with Myra last evening. He disregarded them and rode past and, as he was riding by, he could not help but noticing Freddy's little brothel to his left. Myra was at a window, draped in a black lace negligee, and when she saw him she smiled and waved. Not wanting to be rude, Suresh reciprocated with a slight wave, and Manjula friends, who were watching him like a hawk, had another thing to gossip about.

Suresh knew his actions would be provocative to Manjula's friends, and at this time he was having a bit of fun getting under their skin, and he whistled as he rode off.

He arrived on time at work, and met Abdul at the entrance of the shop. "Good morning," he said to Abdul.

Abdul responded rather insolently, "What's so good about the morning?"

"For one thing, we have sunshine," Suresh said.

"I don't want any backchat from you!" Abdul shouted. "I want you to work on a kitchen table today! And no skylarking, get to it right away!"

Instantly, Suresh became livid, and so started another dreadful day with Abdul.

Suresh went through the cycle of getting angry and laboriously working off his frustrations until he sweated it off, only to have Abdul tick him off again. Just when he thought he could not bear it any longer, that in a moment of aberration he might strike Abdul, Manjula pulled up in her car at the entrance.

When Abdul saw her, his nasty demeanour instantly changed. His face brightened in a broad smile and he rushed up to her with outstretched arms. "Manjula, my gal, what brings you here?" he asked as he gave her a hug.

Manjula gave him a coy smile, and she went on to say, "I need to get a new fridge, the old one broke down this morning. I can't use my car to carry the new one I will purchase as it's not big enough to hold a fridge, can we use your van? And can you take me to the store now?"

It was right in the middle of a work day, but that did not concern Abdul. He dropped his work on the spot and said, "I'd be happy to do so, my sweet gal. Suresh!"

"Yes, Abdul," Suresh answered.

"I'm closing up shop for the day, you can take the rest of the day off," Abdul said, and added, "without pay."

Suresh reacted with a quiet sigh of relief. He was happy that Abdul would never have him work alone in the shop. It was a blessing in disguise at this moment.

Abdul was like putty in Manjula's hands. Whatever she said, whatever she wanted, whenever she did, Abdul would bend over backwards to please her. He hurried Suresh out the door, promising him he would square up his pay the following day as he was busy with Manjula at the moment, and he hastily locked up the shop for the day, in a hurry to ride in the van beside the beautiful and fair Manjula.

Manjula left her car parked there, and she got into the van with Abdul, and as Abdul began steering the wheel to leave, she rolled down the window and hollered at Suresh, saying, "Go straight home and stay there until I get back. Don't go anywhere." She falsely assumed that he would be going out with Myra again.

Suresh did not respond, but after the van pulled away, he got on his bicycle and headed straight home, whistling a tune for he was so happy to have the rest of the day off, away from both Manjula and Abdul.

* * *

At midday, the hot rays of the tropical sun were beating down on the seaside village as seagulls were squawking and playfully soaring above the ocean, dipping down ever so often to catch fish in the glistening water. It was a tranquil day, the warm breeze blowing ever so gently and the waves lapping soothingly against the shoreline.

At this time, three village thieves, Ram the fat man, Eddy the skinny one, and Gopu the short man, were having a *bush-cook* on the shore. They were around the fire, attending to the pot of *cook-up rice* that was boiling, and were gloating over their last thefts.

"We really fooled old Mari," Ram said laughingly, and Eddy and Gopu both burst out laughing, also.

45

"Hey, Ram, you did a good job chatting up Mari and distracting her," Eddy said, repeating the story for about a dozen times. "While you were doing so, Gopu and I snuck in her backyard and entered her fowl coop and snatched the chicken just like that, right under her nose."

"Oh, boy, and them chickens started hollering so loud, I thought Mari would have figured out what was going on," Gopu said.

"I'm so smooth with women, a smooth talker," Ram bragged. "I was telling her how lovely she looked in her bright green cotton frock and her matching headkerchief and pretty bare feet, and I had her smiling and showing off her gold teeth. She was so charmed by my flattery, she didn't notice what was going on with her chickens. I swear old Mari could have dropped her drawers right there and then for me, boy."

Another burst of laughter, and Eddy said, "Man, Ram, you think you're some kind of *starboy* or what?"

"Don't let my fat looks deceive you," Ram said, "I have what they call 'charisma'."

Gopu laughed and said, "If the police were to come after us, I know for sure you would mess your trousers! And there would go your charisma."

"Just hope Mari doesn't figure one of her chickens is missing," Eddy said.

Gopu began gathering up the chicken feathers that were scattered on the shore, of the chicken that was now boiling in the cook-up rice, and he tossed the feathers in the roaring fire. "Best we destroy the evidence," he said.

"Speaking of evidence, I hope old boy Long Fella doesn't find out that we tricked him and stole his *bush rum*," said Eddy

"I told you I'm a smooth talker, man," Ram boasted again. "I was telling him a story about a man who got his rum stolen without him suspecting anything, and there you were, Eddy, right behind his back, pouring Long Fella's bush rum into our bottle and filling his bottle up with water."

Another burst of laughter.

The three of them then went on to contemplate their next theft, contriving a nefarious plan to go to a nearby village this time to steal a duck from another unsuspecting Mari, and bush rum from another gullible Long Fella.

Ram, who was now stirring the pot, went off track, and he asked, "Isn't it somewhere around here that the mad woman lives?"

"You mean the dark-skinned young woman, Seya, who cries all the time?" Eddy asked.

"Yes, man," said Ram, and the Gopu nodded his head.

They looked around but Seya's shack was not in sight, and they shrugged it off for the moment.

After the cook-up rice was finished cooking, they sat around the embers and ate with their fingers, drinking Long Fella's bush rum as they did, and *gaffing* or conversing about this and that. Not too long after they were through eating and were relaxing, a wind started to pick up, carrying the sound of a woman crying.

"Do you hear that? It is the mad woman," said Ram.

"She must be living not too far from here," Gopu said.

"You know that they say she's a witch," said Eddy.

"We should get out of here quickly before she places a curse on us," said Ram, making an attempt to leave.

"Not so fast, you coward," said Eddy to Ram. "Perhaps we can ransack her place for any valuables she may have."

"Nobody from the village wants anything to do with her and we should not go anywhere near to her," said Ram.

"Be a sport, man. Let's go and see if we can steal anything from her," said Eddy.

The three of them eventually all agreed and, now in their inebriated, malevolent state, they set off to find Seya's shack. After walking some distance they found it around a curve of the shore. As they drew closer, they could hear Seya crying even louder now and calling out the name of Mister Gareth. They stormed the shack and found her laying on the floor of the sitting room, a look of fear now registered on her tear-drenched face, her pink cotton sari soiled from rolling around, and her long hair was falling loosely about her.

Eddy poked her with a stick he was brandishing and said, "So you're the mad woman, the witch the villagers are talking about."

Seya shrank against a wall and continued to cry, concealing her face with her hands.

They laughed at her contemptuously and said, "Stupid mad woman."

"Do you have any gold or valuables?" Ram asked.

Seya shook her head.

"Anything to drink, like rum?" asked Gopu.

Seya shook her head again.

They ransacked her place but found nothing of value but a gold-plated comb.

"Where did you get this comb from?" asked Eddy.

It was a comb Mister Gareth had given to her to comb her long black hair, but she did not mention it.

Eddy broke the comb in two and threw it at her, and they all laughed.

"Let's set her place on fire," Gopu suggested.

"This shabby shack is not even worth burning down," said Ram. "Besides, remember we're thieves, not arsonists."

Gopu then said, "We heard you crying and calling out for Mister Gareth. Who is Mister Gareth, your lover?"

Seya did not answer but continued to sob.

"Answer me! Who is Mister Gareth?" Gopu shouted.

When Seya refused to answer, Eddy turned to his friends and asked, "What should we do with her now?"

* * *

At this time, Suresh and Rex had just finished the lunch Suresh had taken in his flask to work that day, and Suresh was now sitting on a chair just outside the shed, peeling a mango with a penknife and throwing the skin to Rex, who wolfed it down greedily. Manjula and Abdul would be gone for the rest of the day, for the refrigerator shop was in a nearby village, so he had the whole of the afternoon off. Confined to the shed, there was not much to do but his favourite thing, so he picked up his mouth organ and began playing some old Indian tunes.

Suddenly, in the middle of playing a sad love song, he had a premonition that something bad was about to happen to Seya. He wanted to go and check on her, but

Manjula, assuming that he would go out and meet up with Myra again, had warned him not to go anywhere before she left. He continued on with the love song, but continued to have that nagging feeling about Seya. Eventually, the feeling that a disaster was imminent was getting too strong for him to ignore, so he thought he would take the chance of venturing to her place, not caring at the moment what Manjula would do if she found out. The consequences he could deal with later. He felt that it was absolutely imperative for him to leave immediately.

He dropped the mouth organ on impulse and left, with Rex by his side this time. His instinct was telling him to hurry but he could only go so fast. Full of trepidation, he raced along the shoreline, his heart beating as fast. Eventually, after what seemed like ages, he came in sight of Seya's shack. As he drew closer, he noticed several footprints on the sand leading up to the stairs of the shack. From the outside, things seemed innocuous, but he shivered at what might be taking place within.

The three men, who had spent the last hour tormenting and mocking Seya relentlessly, were about to assault her when Ram looked out the window and saw Suresh approaching. "Someone's coming, fellows," he said. "I told you that we should have never come anywhere near to this mad woman. I knew she would only bring us trouble."

Eddy peered closely at the man, and said, "It's Suresh, the other good-for-nothing of the village. Don't worry, Ram, the three of us will handle him, no problem." The three of them then rushed out on the verandah to confront Suresh.

A gush of anger seized Suresh at the sight of the men and he picked up a big piece of driftwood and hurried up the stairs to confront them, not caring that he was walking into a precarious situation having to fight off three men. But before he got to the top of the stairs, Rex did and began chasing after the men. The men had heard of the ferocity of the dog, who had maimed a thief who had entered Suresh's shed one night, and, like cowards, they jumped over the verandah and landed on the sand and started running for their lives.

Ram hollered over his shoulder to Suresh, "You good-for-nothing! You and Seya deserve each other."

"You're both are as black as the devil!" Eddy shouted.

"You're both the trash of society!" screamed Gopu.

Suresh let the hard words fall like water off a duck's back. At this point, he really did not care what anyone thought of him, he was only concerned for Seya.

"The witch has got another lover, we heard her calling his name; Mister Gareth," hollered Ram, trying to provoke Suresh.

Suresh did not flinch, but warned: "Don't you ever come around here again! If you do, you would have to battle my dog!" And he threw in, "He's never lost a fight."

The men hurled obscenities at Suresh then fled and went to the village and started to spread the rumour that the two good-for-nothings' were having an affair, and they warned everyone not to venture anywhere near Seya's shack, that she was a mad witch who would put a curse on them. From then on, not a single soul wandered near to Seya's shack. Both Suresh and Seya were shunned and deemed as good-for-nothings'.

As soon as the three men were out of sight, Suresh rushed to check on Seya and found her crouched against the wall, her face contorted with fear, her green eyes reddened with tears. "Did they touch you, Seya?" he asked.

She shook her head and continued to cry as Rex went about sniffing her.

How Suresh wanted to hold her close to him and comfort her, let her lean her head on his shoulders and cry, but when he reached for her, she shrank further away. "I wouldn't let anyone hurt you more than you are, Seya," he promised her, feeling her pain. "I'll leave Rex with you. He's a good guard dog."

"You're very kind to me," she said softly, and made an attempt to stand, but, enervated by the terrible ordeal she had been through, she fell back down and slouched against the wall.

"Stay where you are and rest there for a while," Suresh said. "I'll make you a cup of tea to soothe your nerves." He then went over to the mud stove and lit it and put on a pot of water to boil. He found some lime leaves on the kitchen counter and made her a cup of tea, and he brought it over to her. "Here, sip on this," he said, and he went and got himself a cup, also, and then sat on the old bench across from her, in the sitting room.

Seya sipped on the tea and was silent for a while, then she asked, "Would the men be coming back?"

"I doubt it," Suresh said, "I made it clear to them that if they did they would have to battle my dog. And he's never lost a fight. Trust me, you'll be safe with Rex."

"I'll trust you," she said and breathed a quiet sigh of relief as she looked at the dog sitting by the feet of Suresh.

"I wish I could stay here and protect you, but I must return home. But I'll stay as long as I can."

She did not ask why he had to leave, but said, "I understand."

Suresh then noticed the two pieces of the gold-plated comb strewn on the floor, and he picked them up and handed them to her. "Did the men break your comb?"

Seya took the comb but did not answer, nor did she tell him who had given it to her, and she gathered herself and got up and disappeared in the bedroom and put it away, and when she came back out she began making dinner, while Suresh went out on the verandah and was having another cup of tea as he surveyed the seashore for any sign of the men. As he had said to Seya, he had his doubts that the men would return and he was confident that Rex could handle them, but he still worried about leaving Seya alone.

He took a seat on the chair on the verandah and was sipping his tea as he watched a boat sail by. From there, he could hear Seya cooking in the kitchen, chopping something on a cutting board, and stirring a pot, and she was walking about softly on her bare feet. And, again, he found himself wondering about the story of her life. What really happened to Seya? And who was Mister Gareth? Was he really her lover? And if that were so, where was he? Suresh was falling in love with Seya, he could not deny the fact, and a twinge of jealousy over Mister Gareth suddenly seized him. The feeling dissipated when his mind reverted to having to leave Seya all alone.

53

The sun had just turned gold and it was time for him to leave. He went back inside and found Seya was still cooking. "I must leave now," he said to her.

Seya wanted him to stay for a plate of curried squash and shrimp and rice, but she was too shy to ask. "Thanks for coming to my rescue," she said softly.

"I really wish I could stay," he said again, and as he was about to walk out the door, he whistled at Rex and said, "Sit, my friend." And when the dog sat down, he said, "Stay, stay there, Rex, stay." As he turned to leave, it broke his heart to leave Seya.

Chapter Four

Suresh The Prisoner

The sun was just setting on the horizon of the sea, casting its golden rays on the rippling waves. It was extremely warm on this late afternoon as Suresh hurried along the seashore heading home to his shed, after rescuing Seya. Manjula was not at home as yet when he arrived, thankfully. And Rex was not there to greet him with a wagging tail, and Suresh missed his old friend. He picked up the other source of comfort he had, his mouth organ, and went and sat on the chair outside his shed and began playing a tune, his mind on Seya.

With eyes closed he was lost in thoughts, and above the sound of the mouth organ, did not hear Abdul's van pulling up in the yard, nor Manjula's footsteps racing towards the shed.

"I told you not to go anywhere!" Manjula screamed at him.

Suresh was rudely jerked to an awareness, and he jumped up from his seat and asked, "What are you talking about?"

Flailing her arms, she said, "I stopped in at the local market and it's buzzing with talk that you were at Seya's shack this afternoon." Like the other villagers, she had found out about the mad, crying woman who lived by the seashore.

For all his efforts in trying to keep Seya a secret, Manjula had her way of finding out things, and Suresh's heart sank. "News sure travel fast," he said.

"I thought you had a thing going with Myra," she went on to say, "but I was so wrong."

"You made up a story about me and Myra, Ma, because I came home late one night, and you believed it, and spread it around, and I went along with it just to keep you from finding out about Seya. Sure I saw Seya, but nothing has happened between us."

"I don't believe it. Just like her, you have no class."

The words stung Suresh but he refrained from responding.

Manjula, then noticing that Rex was not around, asked, "Where's the terror?"

"It wouldn't please you to know," Suresh calmly said.

"I'm warning you not to go and see that mad woman again!"

"I can't promise you that, Ma," Suresh said defiantly.

Manjula grew more vexed over this, and said, "The woman is no good for you. I will do whatever it takes to keep you away from her. If I have to hold you here against your will, then I will do so."

"In other words, make me your prisoner."

"Abdul!"

Abdul, who was getting the new refrigerator from his van, immediately dropped what he was doing and rushed up to her side. "What is it, my sweet gal?"

"I want you to take Suresh to work in the mornings and bring him straight home after work."

"As you wish, my sweet gal? When shall I start?"

"Tomorrow morning," she said. "And see to it that you keep an eye on him while he's at work. Make sure he doesn't sneak out at anytime."

She did not really have to instruct Abdul to keep an eye on Suresh, for Abdul always did, watch Suresh like a hawk.

"Anything else, my sweet?" asked Abdul.

"That's it for now," she said.

"I've done nothing wrong but visit an unfortunate young woman, and I don't deserve this kind of treatment," Suresh tried to defend himself.

Abdul thrust his face up at Suresh's at this and clenched his fist, saying, "Shut your mouth or I'll box your ears!"

"Go ahead," Suresh defied, looking him straight in the eye.

"Shut your mouth, I said!"

Suresh sucked his teeth at him which only made Abdul even more irate. "If you do that again, I swear I will give you some good cuffing, which is what you need for being rude."

Suresh refrained from responding this time, but swallowed hard to subdue his anger. It was no use in persisting with this conversation any further, he thought. Abdul had the power to ruin him, sack him from his job as a carpenter, and he would not be able to find work elsewhere in the village, Abdul would make sure of that. So it was wise to keep his mouth shut for now.

Manjula then said to Suresh, "I want you to help Abdul to fetch the refrigerator up to the kitchen."

Reluctantly, Suresh did, and when they came back downstairs, she said to Abdul, "Go home and get me a sturdy padlock for the gate."

Abdul, who lived just five minutes away, rushed home and returned with a padlock and handed it to Manjula. "This should be good enough to keep him inside," he said. The yard was fenced in with metal mesh, and all around was barbwire. With a padlock on the gate, it would be possible but difficult for Suresh to leave the yard.

"That's all for now," Manjula said to Abdul. "You can go home now," she dismissed.

"What about your car, my sweet?" Abdul asked.

With a wave of her hand, she replied, "Leave it parked at the shop for tonight. You can return it tomorrow."

Abdul then got into his van and, when he left, Manjula locked the gate.

"Why are you holding me like a prisoner, Ma?" Suresh asked as she was about to climb the front stairs.

She stopped and now looked at him with such care and compassion in her eyes, unlike the woman she had been just moments ago, and she said, "Honestly, that woman is no good for you, son." He waited for an apology to ensue, and sure enough, Manjula said, "I'm so sorry I have to be so hard on you, my child, but I'm doing this for your own good."

She seemed so sincere at that moment that all Suresh could do then was turn and walk away.

* * *

Manjula stayed home for the next few days to make sure Suresh would not leave to see Seya. As arranged, Abdul picked him up for work in the mornings and dropped him off after work late in the afternoons. Suresh lost his appetite for a couple of days and did not cook, so he worked and went to bed without eating. The third day he cooked a pot of duck curry with rice, all of which he devoured voraciously.

When Abdul dropped him off in the afternoons after work, Manjula was always waiting at the foot of the front stairs to take most of his hard-earned cash. She would then keep him busy, putting him to work around the house, cleaning and dusting her furniture, and cutting the grass in the yard and watering the plants, with her eyes always on his every move.

The weekend arrived and it was midday on Saturday that Manjula was sitting on her verandah watching Suresh labouring in the yard cutting grass. Over the past few days she was angrily ruminating on Seya, obsessed with the thought of Suresh sneaking out again to see her. She could not believe that Suresh would get himself involved with such a woman, she thought, but that was not what was really bothering her, she was afraid Suresh would take off with Seya and she could not stand the thought of him leaving her, like Ranbir and Zara did. Her fury boiled over to the point that she began contriving a plan to pay Seya a visit and put her against Suresh. She waited until Suresh went to his shed to cook lunch for himself that day, and she snuck out.

In the peak heat of the day, she took an umbrella to shield her fair skin from the sun and began making her way along the seashore towards Seya's shack. When she drew close, she noticed that Seya was sitting on a stone with her back to her and was washing some clothes in the sea water, and Rex was nearby, frolicking in the waves. She hid behind a coconut tree and waited, peeping at Seya's every move. After Seya finished washing the clothes, she got up and began wringing them out and placed them in a basin, then she carried the basin over to the clothes line in the back of the shack and hung them all out to dry. Rex was by her side every step of the way.

"Damn dog!" muttered Manjula, "Terror!" She never liked the dog, and it was a mutual feeling, for Rex always sensed her anger and hostility and would bark at her. If he sensed she was there, he could very well foil her plans. In fact, she was sure that the dog had picked up her scent, for he looked over in her direction more than once and barked, and each time he was to leave to investigate, Seya would rub his head affectionately to keep him by her side.

When Seya was finished with hanging out the clothes, she walked over to the little garden she had planted in the backyard and went about picking some chorai callaloo and hot peppers to cook for lunch. Manjula was now growing scared and impatient. She was standing in the heat all that time and was beginning to perspire profusely, becoming enervated. She had no choice, though, but to wait for an opportune moment when Seya and the dog were inside, then she planned on knocking on the door, for there was less chance of the dog attacking her that way. Her wait dragged on much longer than she anticipated, for Seya took the callaloo up to the verandah and took a seat and began snapping the stems and leaves into pieces in preparing it for cooking. Just when Manjula thought she would faint from the heat, Seya finally went inside the shack, with Rex at her heels, and Manjula could hear the click of the door locking.

Manjula waited for a few more minutes to make sure Seya and the dog were not coming out again, then, cautiously, she made her way up the stairs to the verandah, walking as softly as she could to avoid detection. Surreptitiously, she peeped inside through the sheer pink curtain and noticed that Seya was ironing some clothes on the kitchen table with a coal iron, and she had the mud stove lit and a pot was heating up, obviously in preparation for cooking. Then, suddenly, Seya burst out crying and was calling out the name Mister Gareth.

After observing her for a moment, Manjula knocked on the door. Seya got scared right away, thinking it was the three thieves again, but when she looked through the sheer curtain, she saw the outline of a woman. Quickly, she dried her eyes with her green sari veil and went and opened the door.

Rex met Manjula with a menacing growl, and Seya patted the dog on its head to placate him.

Forcing a smile to simulate geniality, Manjula said to Seya, "I need to talk to you."

Seya stepped outside on the verandah, with Rex by her side, and, in a soft voice, asked, "Who are you, and what is it that you need to talk to me about?"

"I'm Manjula, Suresh's stepmother," Manjula said.

"He's never talked about you, neither do I know anything about his life."

"Well, there is something important you should know about him," Manjula said and, without prevaricating, went on to say, "Suresh killed his father when he was a little boy."

The egregious revelation initially brought a surprised look on Seya's face, then she quickly rebounded and said, "I don't believe that for a moment. He's such a kind person."

"My husband is now dead because of him," Manjula went on to say, totally convinced that was true and that she was telling the truth.

Seya then intuitively sensed that, for whatever reason, Manjula was trying to poison her mind against Suresh, and she turned away and was about to go back inside.

Manjula grew frustrated that Seya was not as pliant as she thought she would be, so she decided to take more of a blunt approach, saying, "Suresh is my son and I don't want you to see him anymore, because you're not a good match for him. Break this thing off that you have with him."

"I wouldn't want a step-mother-in-law like you," Seya responded.

"Go back to Mister Gareth."

"What do you know about Mister Gareth?"

"I heard you crying and calling his name. Isn't he your lover?"

Seya broke down and started crying then, and she said, "Just go away and leave me alone, lady. And don't ever come back here again." And she went inside with Rex and bolted the door.

Manjula returned home and went straight to Suresh's shed, and it was then that Suresh found out that she had visited Seya. "I went to see that bad woman, Seya—"

"You did what?" Suresh asked, shocked. "Have you lost your mind, Ma?!"

"No, but I think you have, for the young woman is in love with a Mister Gareth."

Suresh's blood ran hot with jealously over Mister Gareth, and he asked, "She told you that?"

"I heard her crying and calling his name. You should have nothing to do with such a woman. She's the same as Myra. She's a bad woman."

Hurt now arose within Suresh that Manjula was painting Seya as a bad woman, and all he could say at that moment was, "Stay away from Seya, Ma, don't badger her. She's not a bad woman, she's a good person. Don't blacken her reputation like you do with mine. She doesn't deserve this."

"Listen to what you're saying, how could you defend a woman as such? *You* have lost your senses," Manjula said. "It is clear that this young woman is not a decent woman, to be in love with one man and seeing another."

"Let's end this conversation right here, Ma, because you and I don't agree on things."

"Fine," Manjula said. "And if she ends up hurting you and destroying your life, then don't tell me I haven't warned you about her." And with that Manjula left the shed and returned to her house.

Suresh wanted so badly to go and see Seya then. A padlock and a barbwire fence could not really hold him back, for he could easily pick the lock or scale the fence in the middle of the night when Manjula was asleep, but he knew if he did that it would only make matters worse if she found out. So he remained Manjula's prisoner. His mind was at ease, though, that Rex was with Seya to protect her.

His heart sank when Rex returned home a few days later. But he soon found a note tied around the dog's collar with an explanation that put his mind right back at ease again. Ostensibly, another dog, same breed as Rex, a German Shepherd, but a female, had strayed from the seaside village to Seya's shack. Seya took the dog in and named her Rexana, and she wrote she was a good watch dog also. Relieved, Suresh hugged and petted Rex, happy to have his company again. Rex kept Suresh sane, so did his mouth organ.

On the long, hot and lonely nights imprisoned by Manjula, he would lay in his hammock in his shed, with Rex by his side, and play his mouth organ, dreaming of Seya, the evening shadow, for the mere thoughts of her alleviated his loneliness and soothed him like a balm, bringing about sweet equanimity and respite.

Chapter Five

Seya Bathing In The Sea

A month went by since Suresh rescued Seya, and he had not seen her since then. Manjula had Abdul continue to take Suresh to and from work during the week, keeping Suresh on a leash. Abdul would only let Suresh off at the market long enough for him to purchase food, and from there he would take him straight home.

On the weekends, Suresh busied himself with chores around Manjula's house and working in the yard and vegetable garden. On this Saturday morning, he got up early and had breakfast and was having a cup of tea as he was looking out the shed at the rain falling, dreaming of the day when he would extricate himself from the convoluted mess his life was in and become free. He thought of different scenarios of that happening, of just walking out one day and quitting his job, and going into another village and starting life anew, far away from Manjula and Abdul. He dreamed of taking a wife and settling down in a house of his own and having children. Maybe he and Seya could run away together. But that may not be possible if Seya was still in love with Mister Gareth. A pang of jealously struck him then, and he became frustrated over not knowing who was Mister Gareth and where he was at the moment.

The sudden roar of a car engine interrupted his reverie, and he rose and went over to the door to find out who it was at the gate on this early rainy morning. The blue car belonged to Manjula's Uncle Navin, he recognised, and he was honking his horn in trying to wake Manjula to unlock the gate.

Within moments, Manjula came running down the front stairs and, with umbrella in hand, she went to the gate and unlocked the padlock and let her Uncle Navin in.

"Why do you have a padlock on the gate?" he asked Manjula. "Thieves on the loose?"

"Not that alone," Manjula said, "it's Suresh."

"The boy giving you trouble?"

"Never mind him," Manjula said, "what brings you here so early in the morning?"

They came in from the rain and took shelter at the bottom-house, and, from where Suresh was standing, he could see Uncle Navin telling Manjula something. Whatever it was, made Manjula clutch her chest and shake her head, appearing visibly shaken up.

Curious, Suresh left his cup of tea and went to inquire. "What is it, Ma?"

Manjula was now crying, and between sobs, she said, "My mother is very sick. I must go and see her."

Suresh made an attempt to hug her to console her, but she withdrew, so he stood back. "When are you leaving?" he asked her.

Uncle Navin answered, "She should leave right away."

The journey into the village where Manjula's mother resided was a long one, over two hours, and Suresh estimated Manjula would be gone for most of the day. "Should I start the car for you?" he asked, eager to see her go.

"That wouldn't be necessary," Manjula said, "my uncle will be giving me a ride there and back. While I'm gone I want you to dust my furniture and clean my house. I don't want you to leave this place to go and see that bad woman. Do you hear me?" When Suresh did not respond, Manjula added, "Abdul is away visiting his relatives this weekend or I would have him check up on you."

Suresh was relieved to learn of this, but he remained composed.

Manjula went upstairs and quickly got dressed and moments later she returned. Suresh watched in silence as Uncle Navin escorted her with the umbrella to the gate, and when they exited, Manjula locked the gate and got into Uncle Navin's car, and they drove away into the semi-darkness of the morning. Suresh waited until the car disappeared down the street, then he made his way up the front stairs of Manjula's house.

He sat on the verandah for a while, taking in the sights and sounds and smells and activities of the morning as he surveyed the scattered houses on stilts around the neighbourhood. The neighbour to the right was milking a cow at his earthen bottom-house, and his young daughter, a brown-skinned, pretty little dark-haired Indian girl of only three years old, was lingering by the upstairs sitting room window, with her hands propped up on the shelf. Her young mother was in the bottom-house kitchen cooking breakfast on a mud stove, and smoke was floating out the window, the piquant curry scent drifting towards Suresh. The neighbour to the left had a turntable on at this very early hour, and mournful Indian music was softly playing, the vinyl album making a crackling sound, and the plentiful birds were chirping as if singing along to the song. A Blue Saki bird landed on the verandah railing just then and joined in the chorus. And, at this moment, the milk man was on his bicycle delivering fresh cow milk.

Suresh then focused his attention on Neighbour Bertha's house right across the street. Neville and Niles were loading up a basket of fresh vegetables, which they had just picked from their garden, onto a donkey-cart to take to the market to sell.

As Suresh was watching them he could not help thinking about why both men had not gotten married. People said that the older one, Neville, was a bit funny, that he had no interest in women, and Niles could not find a suitable woman for the women he met were too short or too tall, too thin or too fat, too dark or too light, and one who had interest him somewhat was too mouthy for him to live with. Whatever the case, both men were happy and content with the farming life and taking care of their beloved grandmother.

Suresh watched as they covered the produce with plastic and cloaked themselves in raincoats, and they mounted the donkey-cart and began heading off to the market.

As they were passing by, Suresh hollered over at them, asking, "When is Neighbour Bertha returning home?"

"Later today," both men answered.

"Tell her to come and see me when she does."

"We will, man," Neville answered. "Have a good day."

"Have a good day," Suresh reciprocated, and he watched as they disappeared down the muddy street, the donkey-cart jostling them about.

Suresh sat there for a while longer taking in the fresh smell from the various fruit trees in the neighbourhood and watching the rain fall, then when the neighbours began washing their breakfast dishes, he decided to go to work on Manjula's house.

The five-bedroom house, painted white, was ornately furnished in bright colours of red and yellow and green, the bedrooms in fine silk and satin linens, the floors polished in a mahogany hue. Suresh found the dust rag and pinta broom in the closet in the kitchen where Manjula kept them with all her cleaning supplies, and he started out with cleaning the sitting room, sweeping and dusting it to a shine, spic and span. He then tackled the kitchen and did the dishes and the floors, then, leaving Manjula's bedroom for the last, he moved into the other four bedrooms and tidied those too.

He then wandered into Manjula's bedroom and found it in complete disarray; the bed was not made up, clothes and shoes were scattered about, a soiled pink panty was on the floor, a red brassiere was hanging on the bedhead, her cosmetics and perfume on the dresser were uncapped, her comb a tangle of black hair. And the room smelled like it had been slept in for too long; musty. Suresh first opened the windows to air out the room, then he went about making up her bed and hanging up her clothes in the wardrobe, putting her shoes and house slippers on the shoe stand in the corner of the room. After sweeping the floor, he began dusting the ornaments and furnitures in the room, and he paused at the night table to look at the coloured picture Manjula always kept there.

It was a photograph of his father, Raheem, all dressed up in a fine black suit and polished shoes. Suresh sat on the bed and picked up the silver picture frame and stared at the photograph for a while. It was like staring at a slightly older image of himself. His father must have been in his late twenties then, tall and slender with dark skin, a finely handsome visage and a crop of thick black hair. A tear fell from Suresh's eye as he stared into the face of his loving father, and he could not help but thinking how different life would have been for him if he was still alive. A bout of guilt then seized him as he thought of what Manjula would say to him, that he had caused the death of his father. "Sorry, Pa," he said quietly as he ran his fingers over the picture. "It would have been better if the snake had bitten me instead of you. It would have been better for you and me, and Manjula, for she wouldn't have turned out so bitter and angry and depressed, and blame me, and waste her precious life away in grief."

Suresh dwelled on his own hurt feelings for a moment longer as he stared at his father's image, then he went about cleaning the picture frame. As he was doing so, a strand from the rag caught the latch in the back and it came apart, and, to his surprise, he found another picture concealed behind his father's. It was a black and white image of a woman in her early twenties, with prominent Indian facial features; large dark eyes and full lips, a round face with a pair of dimples, and a long braid fell on the front of the bodice of the western frock she was wearing. He turned it over and noticed the name Bhanu was written in blue ink. It was his beloved mother whom his father had told him about when he was just a boy. When she died he was only two years old and could not remember anything about her. Shortly after she had died, Manjula had come into his father's life and Bhanu was so soon forgotten. It was the first time he had seen an image of her, and tears began rolling down his cheeks as he kissed the photograph. He surmised that his father must have hidden it there. Manjula must not have known about this hidden photograph or else she would have destroyed it, he thought. Suresh took the photograph of his mother and put it in his shirt pocket and put together the frame and left his father's photograph where it was. And he finished up with cleaning and tidying the house.

He returned to his shed and hid the photograph of his mother in a metal box where he kept another photograph of his father, among a few things of sentimental value. He then went and had a bath, then picked a *baigan* in the vegetable garden and cooked the eggplant up with some saltfish and rice for lunch, and he and Rex sat down and ate.

It was still raining out now, even heavier. His thoughts then shifted from his parents to Seya. He wondered what she was doing at the moment, if she was still crying and calling out the name Mister Gareth. He began longing to see her, and as he continued to think of her his urge to see her became stronger and stronger by the moment. Manjula was gone and would be for the whole day and if he were to go, she would not find out if he came back on time, he thought, and, he did not have to worry about Abdul dropping in to check on him because he was off visiting relatives. As if the spirits of his parents were guiding him, he found himself getting dressed and ready to leave. Before he did, he picked a bunch of *guineps* from the tree in the yard to take to Seya.

He cloaked himself in a raincoat and then clicked his fingers at Rex, and the two headed to the gate. Picking the lock he thought would be easy, but it turned out to be futile. So he resorted to scaling the wire mesh fence, and in doing so, his cloak was ripped by the barbwire which tore into his arm and created a sharp pain. He bandaged the bloody tear with the raincoat belt and ignored the pain for the moment. Now he had to deal with Rex. Getting him over the fence was not an option. Thinking quickly, he found an opening at the bottom of the fence. Rex was as sharp as he was, spotting the opening just as Suresh did, and the dog slithered his way to the other side.

"Good boy," Suresh said and patted him on the head, and the two then made their way to the seashore.

Manjula's forbiddance of him to see Seya only brought about a greater anticipation for Suresh. His spirit, congruent to the ambiance of the day, soared like the seagulls over the churning ocean, and his heart was singing like the sound of the crashing of the waves and the pitter patter of the rain on the shore. He skipped along on the seashells and broke out in a twirl of Indian dance, and he began singing an Indian love song, his voice sounding above the churning of the ocean. He felt free and wild at that moment, in a state of euphoria. He just could not wait to lay eyes on Seya. And what a thrill he was in for.

When he got to her shack, he found her bathing in the sea in the rain in the sweltering heat of the day. She was fully clothed in a red sari and was washing her ankle-length hair that was floating like black seaweed on the surface of the water. Her sari clung to her shapely, curvy figure like a second skin, and the water on her dark skin was shiny and appealing. She was quite a sight to behold; ravishing. And she almost took his breath away.

"Seya!" he called out to her above the sound of the ocean and the patter of the rain.

She turned and when she noticed him, she quickly placed her arms across the bodice of her sari, but not before he noticed the curve of her alluring young breasts. He watched as she made her way out of the water, and when she reached the shore the waves splashed about her ankles, lifting her sari, and then was when he caught a glimpse of her slender ankles and shapely calves, which made him tingle with excitement.

Shy and embarrassed, Seya hurried by him without saying a word, and she went inside the shack and changed into a dry green sari. Suresh went up to the verandah, and through the swaying sheer pink curtain, he saw her sitting on the floor towel-drying her long black hair, with Rexana by her side. When it was dry, she combed it and let it cascade loosely against her back. Then, like she had done before, she lit the mud stove and began drawing a pot of tea.

The sweet smell of the burning wood, emanating from the mud stove, that seeped through the window of the shack was like incense to Suresh's nostrils, and the heat of the afternoon only added to the amorous charm of the rainy day. He took a seat on the verandah and relished every moment of being there, so close to Seya. And he thought about her bathing in the sea in the rain, an image that was now indelibly etched in his mind. He could not help wondering if, behind her diffident exterior, she had a passionate temperament. And, once again, he found himself wondering about the mystery and eccentricity of her life.

Within a few moments of daydreaming of her, she emerged with Rexana. Rex was thrilled to meet his new girlfriend and began sniffing her, and the two dogs took off and began frolicking on the seashore in the rain.

"I've brought you some tea," Seya said demurely as she set the enamel cup on the table beside Suresh.

"Thank you, my dear. You are so kind to me," Suresh said. "And I've brought you some guineps." And he handed her the bag.

"Thank you," she said as she took the bag, reciprocating, "and you are so kind to me, also." She then retreated in the shack. Moments later, a cry came from within, and the name Mister Gareth. But this time the cry was soft and not as heart-wrenching as it sounded before.

Soon her cries were drowned by a howling wind that swept the waves to the shore in loud crashes. A lightening cracked the sky then and the boom of a thunder was heard. Suresh thought of entering the shack to comfort her, but he knew she would just withdraw with discomfiture, so he sat silently and looked out at the boisterous sea clouded in the dark grey of the sky.

He sat there for more than half an hour and was about to leave when Seya, now dry-eyed, emerged again and asked, "Can I get you another cup of tea?"

"Sure, you can, Seya."

She took his cup and went inside and replenished it and returned, and as she was about to go back inside, Suresh said, "Can you sit with me for just a while?"

Being inhibited, she hesitated at first, then she gathered her sari and sat on the chair beside him, letting her long hair fall to the side against her green sari. She kept her eyes lowered and was toying with the hem of the veil of her sari, and they were silent for a while as the sound of the ocean pulsated and the seagulls squawked.

Suresh stood up then and removed his raincoat, and she looked up then and saw his arm was bandaged with the coat belt, which was soaked in blood. She did not ask what happened to him, but she went inside and came back with a bandage, rubbing alcohol, and a cotton ball. Suresh had sat back down, and, without asking him, she went over to him and began attending to his wound. Her touch was so tender and gentle, and being so close to her made Suresh not mind the sting of the alcohol, in fact, he was tingling with excitement at the touch of her beautiful and small fingers on his skin. He would have loved to have her attend to him longer, but she bandaged him up quickly and took the alcohol and cotton ball inside along with the bloodied coat belt and, shortly after, she returned with the clean belt she had washed. And she took her seat in the chair and remained silent.

"Thank you," Suresh said, "you make a good nurse." When she did not respond, he went on to say, "Ma told me she paid you a visit."

She hesitated for a moment, then responded, "She came here to tell me that you killed your father. And I told her that I don't believe that for a moment." She spoke with her eyes lowered.

Suresh went on to explain the circumstance surrounding his father's death, then he said, "She's been blaming me for it since I was a little boy and I now carry the guilt of it."

"But you didn't do anything wrong and you shouldn't feel guilty," she said, with her eyes still downcast.

"It's something with which I have to come to terms. And sometimes I think the only way I can deal with it is to get far away from her, where she can't put me on a guilt trip. But it's not that easy to leave. I have a job here as a carpenter and very little money saved up, and I wouldn't know where to go from here." He did not bother to explain his situation with Abdul, the other obstacle in his way.

Another silence lapsed, then he decided to broach the subject of the mysterious Mister Gareth. "Now that you know a little about me, tell me, who is Mister Gareth, Seya?"

Lifting her lashes, she met his stare and he noticed the beautiful sea-green of her limpid eyes, conspicuous against her dark skin, and the fine, ethereal beauty of her symmetrical countenance. She did not answer, but averted her head and looked out at the ocean.

Noting her hesitancy, Suresh changed the subject and asked, "Tell me then, where are you from?"

She twirled her long hair around her fingers then, and, eventually, she succinctly answered, "I'm from a nearby village." She spoke so softly, like the sound of a light summer rain, he noticed.

"Where are your parents and family?" Suresh persisted.

"Back in the village."

"Tell me your story, how did you come to live here by the sea?"

She fell silent again for a moment, then, in an emotional voice evincing the pain she was feeling, poignantly answered, "I was thrown out of my home by my parents and six siblings a year ago when I was just fifteen. I'm an outcast."

Suresh commiserated with her, saying, "I'm so sorry to hear this." Then he asked, "What did you do?"

She did not answer but looked askance at him, and he could not help noticing the dejection in her eyes.

"How did you come to live by the sea?" Suresh asked again.

"I had nowhere to go. None of my family or friends would take me in. Then I remembered this abandoned shack that used to belong to my deceased grandfather when he was a fisherman, so I came here."

"What does Mister Gareth have to do with all this?"

She flinched at the question and got up then and went inside, leaving Suresh to assimilate the contents of their conversation. She elucidated certain things of her life, but left him with more questions than answers to muse over. He finished his tea and sat for a while longer, hoping she would return.

She did, and handed him a folded white cotton handkerchief, then she did something she had not done the times before; she smiled at him benevolently. Then she went back inside. Suresh unfolded the handkerchief and found his name embroidered on one end in red thread. A sudden thrill seized him then, and he held the handkerchief to his nostrils and inhaled, taking in the scent of sea breeze mingled with Seya's delicate clean smell.

Suresh waited for a while longer but did not hear any more cries coming from inside the shack. When it was clear that Seya would not return again, he got up and whistled for Rex, and Rex and Rexana came running in from the rain. The dogs did not want to part, but after cajoling Rex, they took off for home.

It was now late afternoon and Manjula was still away when he arrived. He scaled the wire mesh fence, with no mishap this time, and, after helping Rex through the opening at the bottom of the fence, he went straight to his shed. He settled in and cooked *roti* and saltfish for dinner, and he and Rex sat down and ate.

After the scrumptious supper, he settled into the hammock and picked up his mouth organ and he played for a while, imagining Seya as she was bathing in the sea, diving into the abyss of pure bliss at that thought. And the thought of her fingers on his skin, while she was attending to his wound, made him become inebriated with desire for her.

The sound of a revving engine brought him back to reality. Manjula had returned home. Uncle Navin dropped her off and he took off, and she unlocked the gate and padlocked it back again and went straight upstairs. Suresh settled back into the hammock and resumed playing the mouth organ.

It was not before long that he heard Neighbour Bertha hollering, "Manjula! Manjula! Come down and open this gate for me!"

Suresh rushed to the door and looked on, peering through the darkness of the evening.

Moments later, Manjula came down the stairs and stood at the bottom-house.

"What is this?" Neighbour Bertha asked. "Why do you have this gate padlocked?" And she was loud enough for Suresh to hear every word she was saying.

"This is none of your business!" Manjula shouted back.

"It is my business because my friend Suresh lives here!" Neighbour Bertha shouted.

Manjula then said, "I'm doing this to keep him away from that mad woman."

"What mad woman?"

"The young woman who lives by the seaside, Seya."

"But you cannot treat Suresh like this. Have you lost your mind?!"

"Go away!" Manjula screamed.

"I'm not going anywhere! I wouldn't let you treat the boy like a prisoner." Knowing that Manjula believed that she was a fire-rass, she used this as leverage to threaten and scare her. "If you don't open this gate for me, I will seep through your keyhole tonight and suck your blood dry!"

Manjula then began to tremble, and she went to the gate and unlocked the padlock in a hurry.

"Give this lock to me," Neighbour Bertha said, in a headstrong manner, and she took the lock away from Manjula. "If you put another lock on, I will get my grandsons to break it. Do you hear me? And I will come and suck your blood while you're sleeping."

Suresh heard the entire row they had, and he smiled as he watched Manjula scurry up the stairs and shut the door tight, and she turned on all the lights in the house to stave off the fire-rass, for the fire-rass would only come in the dark.

Neighbour Bertha then went directly to his shed. "How long has she held you prisoner?" she asked Suresh.

"Since you left to visit your daughter a few weeks ago."

"Eh, eh, I don't believe this woman!"

"Come in and sit down, and calm yourself down. I'll make you a cup of tea."

Neighbour Bertha entered the shed and took her seat on the peerah on the bare floor, and Suresh went and lit the mud stove and drew some tea and served a cup to her and he got a cup for himself. "Forget about Ma for now. Tell me about your trip," he said, and took his seat in the old armchair opposite Neighbour Bertha.

Neighbour Bertha told of what a wonderful time she had with her daughter, peaceful and restful, and she wanted to stay on a bit longer but she missed her grandsons and had to come back home. Then she was silent for a moment, studying Suresh's face. "I notice romance playing on your burning eyelids," she said. "Are you in love with that young woman Seya?"

Suresh became bashful at her boldness and smiled.

"Would you take her as a wife?"

"I want to, Neighbour Bertha, but she may be in love with someone else."

"I've heard the rumours flying around about her, and I don't believe a word of it. She's a stranger to this village and nobody really knows who she really is."

"I went and visited her today and learned some things about her life, but there are still many unanswered questions."

"Take your time, son, and get to know her. However it turns out, you need to marry a nice girl and settle down. You need a wife in your life."

When Neighbour Bertha left, Suresh lowered the mosquito netting and slipped into bed. He drifted off to sleep that night inhaling the handkerchief Seya had given to him, leaving it beside his pillow.

Chapter Six

The Handkerchief

Early the next morning, while it was still dark out, Suresh woke up to the delicate smell of the handkerchief, and he laid in bed for a moment inhaling it, dreaming of Seya. The indelible and aesthetic image of her bathing in the sea in the rain played on his mind over and over again and evoked passionate feelings within him like an aphrodisiac, and he felt a thrill recalling her beautiful sea-green eyes. He laid there dreaming of combing her ankle-length black hair and running his fingers through it. He was in love with her and only wanted to be around her. But there was Mister Gareth; a man whom Seya had obviously given her heart to. Would he be able to compete with this mystery man and win Seya's love? Perhaps he was already doing so; the handkerchief she had given him was obviously a token of love, and she had smiled at him for the first time. He noted that after she had smiled at him, she went back inside the shack but he heard no more cries coming from her, or the name of Mister Gareth mentioned again. He laid in bed for a moment longer, pondering the brief conversation he had with her. He wondered why she was thrown out of her home and if Mister Gareth had anything to do with it. In spite of his attempt, he had found out nothing about this man. And her life remained shrouded in mystery.

Suresh could have stayed there all morning dreaming of Seya, but the crowing of the fowlcocks and the gentle pawing of Rex eventually got him out of bed, and he left the handkerchief on his pillow and forgot to put the mosquito netting up. His heart was singing as he went about lighting the kerosene oil lamp. He was in love for the first time and he felt like he was walking on air, inebriated with such a wonderful feeling.

"If this is love, then let me go on living," he said to himself. "Yes, there is now a glimmer of hope in my life." And bit of hope for autonomy in his life.

Even the morning air was different now. Yes, it was hot but the warmth only made him tingle now. He even enjoyed the sweat that it brought about. Even the dimness of the oil lamp brought about a coziness, and the darkness of the morning sky seemed to promise him a life of mysteries. The shining stars twinkled down at him, seemingly giving amorous winks. And the auspicious moon was smiling down at him teasingly, like an old friend would do when you are in love. The morning chores of cooking on the mud stove seemed more enjoyable, even the smell of the food and the smoke. And he spent extra long in the cubicle having a bath, drenching himself in the arousing feelings of love.

Rex sensed his feelings and was wagging his tail all along, except, for when Suresh was about to leave for work, when he pulled another trick of hiding his trousers this time.

"Come on, boy, show me where you've hidden my trousers," Suresh said to the dog

Rex gave a small whine, averted his head and sat down, as was his routine.

"I'll be late for work, now go and get me my trousers," Suresh said and got the bag of bone treats.

Rex sat for a while pretending he did not understand, like he would usually do when he was up to his tricks, then, upon another prompting from Suresh, he got up reluctantly and went under the cot where he had hidden the trousers, and he retrieved the trousers and brought and dropped it at the feet of Suresh. Suresh gave him a treat in return, but this morning, Rex was too upset at his master for having to leave that he left the treat on the floor.

"Sorry, pal, I must leave you to go to work now." Suresh said, and he gave Rex an affectionate pat on the head and led him to the door and let him loose in the yard, and he went to the bottom-house to wait for Abdul to arrive.

Manjula then came rushing down the front stairs, still in her nightgown, and barefoot, with her hair in wild disarray. "Have you seen Neighbour Bertha this morning?" she asked frantically.

"I'm sure she's still in bed at this time," Suresh said. "What is it, Ma?"

After her encounter with Neighbour Bertha last evening, when Neighbour Bertha had threatened to suck her blood dry, she had not slept all night, she was so afraid of the fire-rass. And now she felt compelled to cancel out the arrangement she had made in cahoots with Abdul to pick up Suresh for work and bring him home after work, for if Neighbour Bertha learned of this she would put a stop to it by threatening her again.

"I've decided not to let Abdul take you to work or bring you home after work."

Suresh lifted a skeptical brow, and asked, "Why the change of heart, Ma?"

When Manjula did not answer, Suresh figured it out himself with certitude, and he surreptitiously smiled as he went and got on his bicycle and headed off to work. He turned back in time to see Abdul pulling up at Manjula's house to pick him up, and he saw the two of them discoursing, obviously about cancelling the arrangement, and Suresh was sure Manjula would mention the incident of the padlock and Neighbour Bertha being a fire-rass.

As the sky was azure and sunny this morning, instead of going through the seaside village market today, Suresh took his usual route, a long stretch of unpaved road, flanked by a prolific sugarcane field, and he was whistling all the way as he passed cane field workers busy at work, cutting and piling long lengths of sugarcane on to a truck for the sugar factory.

Abdul reached the carpentry shop just as Suresh did, and he did not say anything about the cancellation of the arrangement to Suresh, and for that matter, did not mention the padlock or Neighbour Bertha, for he himself seemed afraid of Neighbour Bertha. So they both went down to work.

The gloom of the dusty carpentry shop did not seem to bother Suresh today, because he was flying high on love for Seya. Abdul barked out succinct orders at him, telling him to do more than one task at a time, but all Suresh did was tackle one at a time and got things done. He did not let Abdul get under his skin. And he did not have to work out anger or grief for he was feeling nothing as such today, and he gladly sawed away at the wood adeptly, sweating drops of happiness congruently, his mind on Seya.

Abdul noticed his happy demeanour and said to him, "What's the matter with you, you don't seem the same today, did you have a romp with Myra last night?"

Suresh did not respond to this.

"Or is it Seya that has caused such a change in you?"

Suresh still refused to respond, but he kept up his happy mood.

* * *

After Abdul left Manjula's place that morning, Manjula sat out on the verandah and was thinking of her ill mother. Her mother had suffered a stroke and was laid up in bed and the doctor told her that it was a matter of time before she would pass away. The thought of another death brought up the memories of her deceased husband, Raheem, and Manjula broke down in tears, crying, and simultaneously cursing God for taking him away from her. She spiralled into the dark hole of grief and no thought could have comforted her. She flew into a rage and went through the house throwing things about and breaking them in her fit of anger, which only resulted in her getting angrier and even more bitter. She worked herself to such exhaustion that eventually she collapsed in bed and succumbed to sleeping, like she would do most of the days of her life, eating very little and languishing away from grief.

She slept through the heat of the day, and woke late afternoon to the bright sunshine pouring through the open window. She got up and cleared away the broken pieces of ornaments she had shattered, then she went out on the verandah and sat there.

She ruminated on Raheem for a while, still missing him after all those years and becoming angry over her situation. Then her mind turned to Suresh; she had a sneaky suspicion that he had snuck out again to see Seya, which only fuelled her anger. Suresh's shed was always left unlocked, so she decided she would go and take a look around to see if she could find any clues. Rex met her with a menacing growl as she was heading into the shed, but that did not deter her, she walked passed the dog and opened the door and entered.

The shed was in semi-darkness and was hot as usual. She looked around and sensed that something was amiss; Suresh always kept the place tidy and immaculate, the dishes washed, kitchen table wiped clean, floor swept clean, but, today, the mosquito netting above the cot was left down. As she was heading over to the cot, she noticed a metal box by the side of the bed, where Suresh kept his father and mother's pictures and things of sentimental value. Fortunately, Manjula mistook this box for a tool box, so she left it alone. She then lifted the mosquito netting from the cot and immediately noticed Seya's white cotton handkerchief on the pillow. Picking it up, she noticed the name Suresh embroidered on it.

"Leave that alone!" Suresh had just arrived from work and caught Manjula just then with the handkerchief in hand.

"Who gave this to you?" she demanded to know, holding the handkerchief aloft and brandishing it about, an austere expression registered on her face.

"That's none of your business, Ma," Suresh said.

"That bad woman gave it to you, didn't she? So you went and saw her again! Didn't I warn you not to do so!" Manjula shouted, behaving in a blackguard manner.

"Just give it to me," Suresh pleaded.

"So you did see her and she gave you this handkerchief," Manjula said, and flung the handkerchief at him. "I'm warning you again not to ever see that woman again!" she added emphatically.

"Or else?" Suresh asked as he caught the handkerchief. And when she did not answer, he went on to say, "Why don't you take a stick and beat me, Ma? Maybe it would take away some of the anger and bitterness in you. Or, better yet, why don't you just drive me away from your home?"

Manjula flopped onto the cot and held her head and started crying then. "You're the reason that my husband is dead!" she said, "and I should have nothing to do with you, but I need you now."

"I'm nothing more than a sack of rice punchbag to you, Ma. You don't need me. What you need is to deal with your anger and grief. Your two children have left you, but I've stayed behind because I feel sorry for you, because I'm also hurting and grieving over the death of my father. And I so need a mother and hope that someday you would be a mother to me, like you used to be before Pa died. But all you do is mistreat me and take your frustrations out on me, like you've done to your own children. Maybe someday, when I can't take it anymore, I, like your children, would gather the courage and leave also, leaving you to wallow alone in your misery."

"You mustn't leave me, Suresh," Manjula then pleaded.

"Then let me live my life. Give me the freedom to see Seya."

"I wouldn't let you see that bad woman again. She's no good for you, son. The whole village is saying that she's a witch and that she's got another lover, a Mister Gareth."

"Go up to the house and leave me alone now, Ma," Suresh said, fed up with her abuse and control, and the mention of Mister Gareth as Seya's lover only infuriated him and made him jealous, so he saw no need in expostulating with her any further.

Manjula got up and started making her way out the door, saying as she did, "You can't leave me, Suresh. You've got nowhere to go and you'll have no job. You can't survive without me." Then suddenly, she fainted and collapsed.

Reflexively, Suresh caught her in his arms before she hit the ground, and, her being as light as a feather from wasting away, he had no problem carrying her up the front stairs to her sitting room, where he laid her out on the sofa. He got some Limacol from the medicine cabinet and soaked a handkerchief and tied it around her head, and within a few moments Manjula stirred.

"What happened?" she asked.

"You fainted and collapsed," Suresh answered. "Did you eat at all today?"

"I've eaten just a mouthful or so."

Suresh went and warmed up some soup for her and brought her a bowl. "If you don't change your ways, you will end up dying of fatigue and exhaustion, Ma" he said to her.

"I cannot help myself," she said. "I'm so down that I don't even care if I live or die."

"Don't talk like that, Ma."

"Even sleep is evading me now. I haven't slept in a couple of days."

"I'll go to the drug store and get you some medication to sleep," Suresh offered, and he left her and got on his bicycle and headed off to the drug store in the seaside village. The pharmacist recommended a sleeping pill, and Suresh purchased it with his own money and he hurried back home.

As soon as he returned, he drew Manjula a bath and made a cup of tea for her and gave her the pill to drink, and he tucked her into bed. He then pulled up the chair next to the bed and sat there, watching her pitifully.

"What the hell are you staring at?" she asked him cantankerously.

"I love you, Ma," Suresh said.

Manjula's eyes were now getting heavy with sleep, and just before she drifted off, she responded in a contrite manner, "I love you, too, son."

Suresh sat there a little longer and watched her as she was sleeping and he thought of how peaceful and innocuous she appeared. He only wished she could be the same way when she was awake. When she began snoring, he got up and left, leaving the lights on so if she woke she would not be afraid of being in the dark and dreading being attacked by the fire-rass.

When he returned to his shed, he sat down in the old armchair and broke down and started crying, drying his eyes with the handkerchief Seya had given to him. He felt torn between his visceral feelings for his stepmother and the woman with whom he was in love. Manjula was wrapped up in her grief and anger and bitterness, so much so that she was oblivious to the fact of how much hurt she was causing him.

Rex sensed the sadness of his master and he pawed at Suresh and jumped up and licked the tears from his face.

"I'll be all right, boy," Suresh said to him and rubbed his head. The dog then went over to the night table and picked up the mouth organ with his mouth and brought it to Suresh to cheer him up. "Okay, I'll play us a tune," Suresh said to him.

Suresh began playing an Indian love song on the mouth organ, and in that moment his pain and grief that had returned, dissipated. If it were not for Rex and the mouth organ alleviating his sufferings like a good antidote or balm, his life would be unbearable, he thought, and he let himself be immersed into a world of calmness to the tune of the song.

Chapter Seven

Fishing By The Seaside

A warm wind accompanied by overcast skies brought in the next morning. Suresh slept in as it was Saturday morning, a day off work. When he awoke he clutched the handkerchief Seya had given to him, and he laid in bed a while longer thinking of her. His morning-dreaming of her was soon interrupted by Rex gently pawing him to get up.

"Okay, old boy, I'll get up and make us breakfast," Suresh said to the dog as he hauled himself out of bed, and he went about lighting the kerosene oil lamp. He then lit the mud stove and put on a pot of water to boil, and he went in the garden and picked some lime leaves and brought it back and made himself some tea.

He went outside and sat on the chair in front of the shed, and was enjoying his tea while taking in the dreamy atmosphere of the early morning. Manjula was still asleep at this time, but the neighbours were up and were already busy with their morning chores. You could hear the sounds of someone chopping wood, pots and pans clanging, a baby crying, and the bray and moos of the animals around. A cock and a hen, the neighbour's chickens, had entered the yard through the hole at the bottom of the mesh fence, and the cock was chasing the hen around the yard. Suresh got up and drove them out of the yard and he plugged the hole in the fence just as a mother duck and her six yellow ducklings were trying to get in.

He returned to the shed and finished his tea, and then he went about making roti and saltfish for breakfast, and he and Rex sat at the table and ate. As they were doing so, he heard the sound of the wheels of a vehicle crawling up the street, and Suresh left his breakfast and went outside to inquire who it was.

Manjula's uncle, Navin, came to a stop at the gate and he stood there hollering, "Manjula, Manjula!"

Manjula, who had somewhat recuperated from her fainting incident last evening, was still very weak, and she dragged herself out of bed and went over to the sitting room window and asked, "What is it, Uncle Navin?"

"Your mother is now very, very sick and I've come to take you to her," Uncle Navin said. "Pack a few things to stay for a week."

Suresh then interjected, "Ma is not feeling well herself, Uncle, I don't know if she can take the travelling."

"It's a very dire situation, and her mother really needs her now," said Uncle Navin.

"I will go," Suresh could hear Manjula saying from the window above. "Just give me some time to get dressed, Uncle."

Suresh rushed upstairs and found Manjula in her nightgown, looking ashen-faced and sickly. "Let me accompany you along," he offered her.

"That wouldn't be necessary, I will be gone for a week and you have to go to work," Manjula said.

"Uncle Navin will be with me should I faint again."
And in a voice as tender as she was when she had told
him she loved him last evening, she said, "No need to
worry, son." And she went and had a bath and began to
get ready.

Suresh helped her to pack a suitcase of clothes and
toiletries as she was doing so, and he went to the shed
and brought some of his breakfast for her. "You must
put something in your stomach before you leave, Ma."

"I'm not hungry."

Uncle Navin, who had joined them upstairs, said,
"Eat something, my niece. It's bad enough that my
sister is gravely ill, and I can't bear the thought of you
getting sick also."

Reluctantly, Manjula sat down at the kitchen table
and had a few morsels of food. And she said to Uncle
Navin, "Take the suitcase down to the car, I need to
speak to Suresh alone." When Uncle Navin left, she
said, rather emphatically, to Suresh, "As you know, I
will be gone for a week, and while I'm gone I don't
want you to go anywhere. You're not to go and see that
bad woman. Do you hear me?"

Suresh let out an agitated sigh. He wished she would
not bring up Seya. He was starting to feel good about
her after she told him she loved him, and now she was
back to her controlling, austere ways. "Go and take care
of your sick mother and don't worry about me, Ma," he
said, as he tried to control his agitation.

"You better do as I say, or else—"

"Don't threaten me, Ma. I'm not a little boy that you
can push around. I'm getting tired of your threats."

Before she could react, Uncle Navin came back
upstairs and took her by the arm and said, "Let's go

94

now. The faster we leave the sooner we will get there. The old lady is waiting for you." And with that, Uncle Navin took her to the car and, before they started their journey, Manjula asked Uncle Navin to drop in on Abdul.

"I'm on my way to visit my sick mother and will be gone for a week," she said to Abdul. "I want you to keep an eye on the boy, and make sure he doesn't visit that bad woman, Seya." With that said, she and Uncle Navin left.

Suresh stayed home that day and all weekend, and the next week he bicycled to and from work. It turned out to be the most peaceful week he had had. Manjula was not around to nag him and accuse him of killing his father, and it was pleasant to have a break from her.

Abdul did what he was told and kept an eye on Suresh. He dropped in on him often on the weekend Manjula left, and made it his duty to check up on him in the following weekday evenings, making sure he was staying at home and not going anywhere near to Seya.

From across the street, from her verandah, Neighbour Bertha had been observing Abdul as he came and went on the weekend and the following weekday evenings, and she suspected something was not right. She always had an aversion to Abdul and wondered what he was up to. When Suresh came home after work on the Friday she decided to pay him a visit to find out what was going on.

Suresh was busy cooking a pot of cook-up rice for dinner when she arrived, and he said, "Come in and have a seat, Neighbour Bertha." She entered the shed and took her seat on the peerah on the floor, a look of concern on her face. "What's troubling you, Neighbour?" he asked.

"I haven't seen Manjula for a few days now, where is she?"

"She's visiting her mother who is very sick."

"And she left Abdul to watch-man you, right?"

"Ma's afraid I would visit Seya again, so she asked Abdul to check up on me."

"I don't believe that woman, still treating you like a prisoner."

Just then Abdul showed up to check on Suresh, and Neighbour Bertha got up and met him sharply at the shed entrance with a baleful stare. "What are you doing here?" she asked.

"Just checking up on Suresh," Abdul said.

Neighbour Bertha placed her hands on her hefty hips, and she exploded, "What are you, Manjula's watchman? Eh, eh, what do you take this young man to be, a child that you should be watching over him? You take your eyes and pass him." Then flailing one arm, she continued with saying, "Clear yourself out of here at once, you beast!"

Abdul was taken aback and was left speechless, afraid to contend with a fire-rass as Neighbour Bertha was rumoured to be.

Old Neighbour Bertha then picked up the cricket bat that Suresh kept at the entrance of the shed, and she opened the shed door and began chasing after Abdul, and Abdul ran, like a coward, out the gate. "If you come back here again, I will pay you a visit in the night and suck your blood dry!" she threatened.

Abdul quickly got into his van and hurriedly started the engine and, before driving off, said, "I've got a message for Suresh."

"What is it?" asked Neighbour Bertha.

"Manjula called me today and said she won't be returning home tomorrow but on Monday."

Suresh heard him, but Neighbour Bertha said, "I'll tell him. Now, you be on your way and don't let me see you around here on the weekend or anytime. Do you hear me?"

"I heard you," Abdul said and sped away as fast as he could. And Neighbour Bertha returned to the shed.

Suresh could not help smiling. The power Neighbour Bertha had over both Manjula and Abdul, an innocuous old woman whom they superstitiously believed was a fire-rass, who used this to her advantage to intimidate. "You old fire-rass," he teased.

Neighbour Bertha broke out in a smile herself and began cackling. "I've taken care of him. You wouldn't be seeing him around here anymore, I can assure you. He wouldn't badger you anymore."

"If Abdul is Ma's watchman, then you are my protector," Suresh said.

Neighbour Bertha then took her seat back on the peerah, and Suresh dished her out a hot plate of cook-up rice, and a plate for himself, and he sat beside her on the bare floor and they began eating with their fingers.

"Enough of this nonsense that you can't visit the gal," Neighbour Bertha said. "You have my permission to do so."

"But if Ma found out she will be very vex with me," Suresh said with apprehension.

"Let her be vex and spoil her own face," Neighbour Bertha said. "But I wouldn't sit around and condone her behaviour and have you be taken advantage of. She can't have you tied to her apron string for the rest of your life. If you're in love with this gal, then go and see her. You have my blessings."

* * *

The next day was blisteringly hot in the seaside village and villagers were busy with the weekend chores. The beating of clothes was heard somewhere in the vicinity as others were scrubbing their stairs. It was lunchtime now, and pots and pans were clanging, as smoke rose from the mud stoves of those cooking, releasing appetising whiffs of curry spice.

Instead of cooking lunch today, Suresh got on his bicycle and went into the village and treated himself to some *lo mein* at a Chinese restaurant, then he went to the market, looking for a gift for Seya. A vendor at a stall was selling hair clips and combs and cosmetics and jewellery, and toiletries for women, and Suresh stopped by. Manjula's coterie of garrulous girlfriends at the market leaned into each other's ears and were whispering when they saw him, but he paid them no mind.

"I want to buy a gift for a friend," Suresh said to the vendor, who was a small-statured man, about fifty years old or so who was fairly new to the village.

The vendor smiled at him and asked, "For a girlfriend?"

"No, no," Suresh said. "But she's someone very special."

"Well I have a nice bracelet here, and here's a beautiful comb, and here's a gold chain. Do you have anything in mind, young man?"

"I want something sweet, something sensual," Suresh said.

"You're sure this is not for a girlfriend?" the vendor asked.

"I only wish," Suresh said.

"I have a beautiful little bottle of perfume that is very sensual," the vendor said, and got a small purple bottle and showed it to him. "You can test the scent."

Suresh opened the ornate gold cap of the little purple bottle and sprayed a touch on his wrist and inhaled the scent, and he said, "Very sensual. I think she'll like it. I'll take a bottle."

He paid for it and placed it in his trousers pocket, and as he was turning to leave, he encountered Myra the prostitute, all dressed up in a hot red frock and matching heels, with her black hair flowing down her back. "I noticed you buying a bottle of perfume," she said, "is it for me, darling?" Manjula's girlfriends were craning their necks now to take a peek at the exchange between her and Suresh.

Suresh did not answer.

From Manjula's girlfriends point of view, they could only see the back of Suresh now, and Myra was obscured behind him, and they surmised that Suresh had given the bottle of perfume to Myra. "Imagine that," said one of them, "he's seeing that mad woman by the seashore and he's giving the prostitute a bottle of perfume. What kind of man is this? Disgusting! And to think that Manjula has to put up with his wicked behaviour."

"Well, if the gift is not for me, then who is it for?" Myra asked.

"Never mind," Suresh said. "I must be on my way."

"She's one lucky woman," Myra said. And, as he was riding off on his bicycle, she said, "Wait!"

Suresh stopped, and asked, "What is it?"

"I've been seriously thinking about what you said to me the last time I saw you, when you said for me to go home and think about what you told me, that I'm disgracing my family and myself, and, that why I should waste my life when I could have settled down with someone decent and have a respectable life."

"And?"

"You see, I couldn't leave Freddy," she said, referring to her pimp, "because he had threatened to kill me if I did. But things have changed now."

"How so?"

"Freddy had a heart attack and died, and now I'm free."

"What would you do now?"

"I've been shopping for some new clothes to sport more of a modest look. Now I'll move to Suriname and start a new life."

"You're still young and beautiful, I'm sure you can attract a husband there."

"I will be staying at my Auntie's house, and she will be matching me up with the son of one of her friends." Then after a pause, she added, "Thanks for taking the time to talk to me about my life. No other man has ever bothered to do that, they all wanted to use me."

"I'm glad I was able to talk some sense into you. I hope you find what you're looking for," Suresh said, and as he was riding off bid her, "Goodbye, Myra."

"Goodbye, sweet man," Myra said, and went her way as Manjula friends looked on.

Suresh went back home and left his bicycle, and he and Rex headed to the seashore, racing towards Seya's shack. When they arrived, Rexana met them, wagging her tail in the delight of seeing Rex, and the two dogs took off playing on the seashore.

Seya, who lived off the land and sea, was in the water fishing with a net when she saw Suresh, and she said, "I had a feeling you'd come by today."

Enamoured of her, her reaction immediately put him in an ebullient mood, and he said, "Ma is visiting her mother and she will be away until Monday, so I took the chance of stealing this opportunity."

"Come then, help me to catch some *bangamary* fish and shrimps for dinner."

Suresh removed his shirt and trousers and waddled in the water and met her. Seya was in a pale yellow cotton sari that accentuated her dark skin and green eyes, and it clung to her seductive curves. "You look so beautiful," Suresh said to her, beaming from ear to ear.

Lowering her long lashes, Seya smiled. It was evident she was as happy to see him as he was of her. "Thank you," she said.

"It would be better if we used a hand-seine to catch fish, do you have one?" Suresh asked.

"Yes, I do. Wait here and I'll be right back with it." Seya got out of the water, carrying the fish net, and she got the hand-seine net from the bottom-house of the shack and returned.

"Take one end, and I'll hold the other," she said as she met him in the water.

They dragged the hand-seine net through the water, and within a few moments pulled it up on shore. And what a copious catch they had. The bangamary fish were glistening in the sun, fresh and alive, and so were the shrimps, jumping and twisting and turning.

"I'll curry the fish and fry the shrimps with some chorai callaloo," Seya said, and, now, becoming a little less shy, asked, "Would you stay for dinner?"

Without hesitation, Suresh answered, "Sure, I would love to. And I'll help you to clean the catch."

"Okay."

While Seya went inside the shack and changed into a dry blue sari, Suresh sat at the edge of the shore and cleaned the catch. Afterwards, he washed up in the sea and put his shirt and trousers back on. He then went up to the verandah and peeked inside and found Seya in front of her shrine saying a prayer. This time, though, she did not cry or call out the name Mister Gareth. In fact, when she was through with her prayer, she greeted him with a demure and benevolent smile at the door.

"I've brought the cleaned catch for you to cook," Suresh said to her.

She took the bowl but did not invite him in, instead, walking softly in her barefoot, she retreated to the kitchen and lit the mud stove and put on some tea to boil. She returned moments later and brought him a cup and she went back inside, leaving him on the verandah to sip on it while she went about grinding up curry spices on the masala brick, sitting on the bare wooden floor as she did. When she was finished, she went in the garden and picked some chorai callaloo to cook with the shrimp, and she returned and began cooking.

Sitting on Seya's verandah was a pleasurable moment for Suresh in its relaxed ambiance, which was congruent to his emotions at that moment. He looked out at the golden sunshine beating down on the glistening waves and heard the soothing lapping of the water on the shore, and the call of the birds. This afternoon, the sky was azure with soft white clouds floating by, but it was as hot as an oven. Seya had turned the radio on, and he could hear Indian love tunes sailing out the window. Caught up in the moment, Suresh fancied himself living such a life with a wife by his side, and the two dogs playing along the shore and, perhaps, a few children of his own. If only his dreams would come true, he thought. He remained there, dreaming of building a house and using his carpentry skills to make his own furniture, seeking autonomy for his life and building citadels in the air.

The sizzling of the melange of spices caught his ears as Seya began cooking, the piquant scent drifting through the open window of the shack. That and the scent of rice boiling and shrimps frying with the chorai callaloo caught his nostrils, and soon he was salivating with hunger. He wondered if Seya would invite him inside to eat, and his answer came shortly after when she emerged with an enamel plate of steaming food and a cup of water and a bottle of mango *achar* condiment.

"Eat it while it's hot," she said and turned to leave.

"Wouldn't you join me on the verandah?" he asked.

She hesitated for a moment, then said, "Okay, I will."

She brought her plate of food and cup of water, and they ate hungrily with their fingers without saying a word, Seya lapsing into her silent, inscrutable mode, but stealing clandestine glances at him whenever he looked down at his plate, not realising that he could sense it. Suresh wanted so much to talk to her, find out more about her life, but he sensed she was shy and hesitant to say much, so they ate in quietness and enjoyed the scrumptious dinner as the sun was beginning to set on the horizon, casting its golden rays about. When they were finished, Seya went inside and washed her hands in the dish sink, and she brought out a basin of water for him to wash his, and a flour bag towel for him to dry them. Then she went back inside and made some vermicelli milk pudding, and they enjoyed that out on the verandah, also, in silence.

After they were finished, Seya rested the bowls on the side table, then Suresh said to her, "I've bought you a little gift." And he took the little purple bottle of perfume from his trousers pocket and handed it to her.

Seya's sea-green eyes lit up, and she smiled and said, "Perfume. You make me feel so special, Suresh."

The sound of his name on her lips rolled out so smoothly and sounded so sweet to his ears. "My pleasure," he said, and took pleasure out of seeing Seya smiling and holding the bottle of perfume so preciously. "I'd like you to try it on for me."

"I will do so after I bathe in the sea," Seya said, and she took the bowls in and washed the dinner dishes.

She then called the dogs and fed them some of the food, and after the dogs went back out to play, she went to bathe in the sea in her sari, while Suresh watched her from the verandah in awe of her ethereal beauty. He could not help thinking of how pleasant Seya appeared now, not like the crying mad woman he had known when he first met her. The sadness or madness of Seya was being cured and he knew his company had something to do with it. Maybe, she was falling in love with him also. If only that were so, he thought to himself as he watched her bathing so alluringly.

She came back inside when she was done and got dressed in a dry green sari, and she stayed inside and sat on the floor and towel-dried her hair. Moments later, she lit the mud stove again and made tea, and she brought it out to him, as well as a cup for herself, and she took a seat on the chair beside him.

The sun in the opalescent sky had just turned to a reddish-gold, casting its rays on the rippling waves of the sea, and the place was just a little less warmer, the breeze blowing about with merely lackadaisical strength.

"I'll try on the perfume now," she said to Suresh as she went about opening the cap of the bottle. She sprayed a bit on her wrist and inhaled it and said, "It's so sensual. I love it."

"That's what I thought, too."

She then sprayed some on her neck below her ears, and had fun taking in the scent. Leaning close to Suresh, she said, "Do you like it on my skin?"

Suresh leaned forward and smelled it, and for a moment, he felt like embracing her and kissing her, but he quickly dismissed the thought and said, "It's heavenly. It just suits you, Seya."

The intimacy of the moment made Seya shy, and she withdrew without saying another word and went inside.

By now dusk was falling, dusty-blue over the tranquil sea, the twinkling stars emerging in millions, a full moon casting its rays about. And Seya lit the kerosene oil lamp within. Suresh ensconced himself in the hammock and was relaxing on the verandah, and he found himself not wanting to leave this bit of heaven and peace he had found, like an oasis in a barren desert. He remained there until the lamp in the shack went out, and not too long after he fell asleep, drifting into a beautiful dream of him and Seya running hand in hand through a field of flowers.

Seya, who had fallen asleep herself, woke up to Suresh slapping off the mosquitoes biting into his skin, and she got up and found him sleeping in the hammock. She lit a mosquito coil and placed it beside him, and she covered him with a blanket, then she went back to sleep in her room in the shack, leaving Suresh to spend the night there.

Chapter Eight

The Final Straw

In the semi-darkness of the next morning, Suresh stirred to a gentle warm breeze caressing his face and the sound of waves washing up on the shore, the cacophony of seagulls squawking. At first, he was disoriented, thinking he was having a morning dream of being at Seya's place, but when he opened his eyes he found himself in her hammock on the verandah. He had obviously fallen to a sound sleep last night and spent the night there. He noticed he was covered in a blanket and just nearby was a mosquito coil that was now burnt down to ashes, and a smile crossed his lips that Seya was so kind to take care of him while he was sleeping.

He got up and peeked inside the shack, but it was still dark, which appeared that she was still sleeping. He oscillated between waking her and leaving, then eventually thought it best to let her sleep and he should be on his way. Rex was also fast asleep, cuddled up beside Rexana on the verandah, and Suresh gave a low whistle and woke him up, and the two were soon on their way home.

Suresh felt a sense of euphoria as he was strolling along the seashore. The day and night spent at Seya's place was the most pleasurable time he had had in his life. Just to see her and be by her side was a thrill. He ruminated on her smile and the benevolence she had shown him. She did not cry this time at all, neither did she call out the name Mister Gareth, he noted. Could it be she was falling in love with him now? He clung to that hope as he hurried along.

He was so lost in thoughts of Seya that before he knew it he was nearing home. Just as the sight of the house came into view, he saw Uncle Navin pulling away in his car; Manjula had obviously returned a day earlier than expected. And now Suresh dreaded the thought of having to encounter her.

She was at the bottom of the front stairs when he entered the yard, and straightaway she pugnaciously went on the attack and shouted, "You spent the night with that bad woman! Shame on you!"

"It's not what it seems like, Ma. I just fell asleep on her verandah," Suresh started to defend himself.

"I wasn't born yesterday. I know what you two were up to!"

"Don't be so sure, Ma."

"Didn't I warn you not to go to her place? If you ever do so again, I will cut your tail!" she threatened.

"Beat me like you did when I was a child," Suresh lashed back angrily. "I've told you over and over again, and I'm telling you again, Ma, someday you will lose me."

"I wouldn't allow you to leave me."

"You can't stop me either."

Manjula then broke down in a deluge of doleful tears, playing on Suresh's tender side, and she said, "What would I do without you? My husband's dead, my children have left me, and now my mother's dying. And I fear living alone in my grief and misery."

The anger that Suresh was feeling towards her dissipated at the sight of her crying so pitifully and looking so weak and delicate, and he said, "Perhaps you need time alone to deal with your grief and misery."

"You wouldn't leave me, Suresh, would you? I need you now more than I ever did."

Suresh did not respond to that but took her gently by the arm and began leading her up the stairs, saying, "Come, let me make you a cup of tea to soothe your nerves."

He sat her down on the sitting room sofa and brought her a handkerchief to dry her tears, and he went about making her a cup of tea, and served it up to her. As she sipped on the tea her sobbing subsided and she became calm. Worn to a frazzle by her grief and fear, she eventually became drowsy and she stretched out on the sofa and succumbed to sleep, and Suresh brought her a pillow and placed it beneath her head and he left.

He then got Rex and went and sat under a mango tree in the backyard and tried to sort things out in his mind. Manjula's threat to beat him was more than he could take. She had incessantly bad-mouthed him all his life over the death of his father, and he had to live with the ignominy and guilt and ostracism for all these years, and as a child he had clung to her and was still doing so in hoping she would change someday, but she was incorrigible and all he was doing was deluding himself, he sadly came to that realisation. He wondered if he were to leave her where he would go. He had no one to turn to; no other family or friends, except, for Neighbour Bertha who would gladly take him in, but that was not an option for he would still remain too close in proximity to Manjula. And he wondered if he lost his carpentry job with Abdul, what would he do then? He was in a predicament.

As to marrying and settling down with a wife, what was the chance of that happening? He was in love with Seya, but he was also deluding himself, he thought, for there was Mister Gareth, who may or may not be alive, a man whom Seya was seemingly connected to romantically. But was she really? What was her connection with this man? And, more importantly, what kind of a person was she? Was she really a bad woman like Manjula had said, or a mad woman like the villagers rumoured, or was she just an outcast like himself, a person born to misfortune and mistreatment? He really did not know much about her except that she was thrown out of her home. He knew not why and what had happened in her life. What terrible act had Seya committed that had caused her life to go awry?

Since he met her, he momentarily had glimpses of a different life, a good and settled life with a wife and children, but he was left with the reality of his present circumstance. The more he thought of his life in trying to sort things out, the more things became complicated to him. And he was now growing more and more frustrated with each moment that passed.

The gentle pawing of Rex on his arm brought his attention to the dog, and he broke out in a smile immediately. "You give me reasons to go on, old boy," he said to the dog. "You're my best friend, Rex. What would I do without you?" And he petted the dog on his head.

Rex wagged his tail and led him to the shed and got the mouth organ and brought it to him. The dog knew just what to do to cheer him up, and Suresh took the mouth organ and started playing an Indian love song. And just like that, his worries seemed to take wings and left him for the moment.

He then went about lighting the mud stove, and made roti and saltfish for breakfast. After he and Rex ate, he got his cutlass and took to cutting the grass in the yard, a chore that took him most of day. Late in the afternoon, as the sun was just setting, Uncle Navin came calling at the gate.

Manjula met him at the bottom of the front stairs and he broke the news to her: "Your mother has passed away, my niece."

"Ma has left me also!" Manjula cried, and flung her arms about. "What is happening to my life?" Uncle Navin held her and tried to comfort her, but Manjula was full of pity for herself and went on bawling, "What is happening to me? What would happen to my life now? Suresh, where is Suresh?"

Suresh dropped the cutlass with which he was cutting the grass and went to her. "What is it, Ma?"

"My mother is dead, my father long died, and my husband is dead, what is happening to my life? What would become of me? You wouldn't leave me, Suresh, will you?"

"Your mother is now dead and you should be grieving her loss instead of thinking of yourself," Suresh said. "What would happen to you depends solely on what you decide to do with yourself."

Uncle Navin said to her. "We should leave now and go and arrange the funeral."

"I'll come along," Suresh offered.

"No, you have to go to work," Manjula said.

Suresh did not persist; he had never met Manjula's mother and had no attachment to her. "Okay, I'll stay behind and go to work," he concurred.

"I will be gone for a few days, and while I am, don't go anywhere," she said emphatically. "Don't go and see that bad woman again."

"That should be the least of your worries at the moment, Ma," Suresh said. "Attend your mother's funeral and grieve her loss."

"Another funeral," Manjula cried, then in a voice brimming with acrimony spewed, "You killed your father, Suresh!"

Anytime he heard that, it was like opening a sore wound, but today it was worse than that, it felt like a stab to Suresh's heart. And all of a sudden he found the courage to finally stand up for himself. In an assertive voice, he said, "I've come to the end of my rope, Ma, this is the final straw, you've pushed me too far, I'm fed up, and this is as much as I can take. I did not kill my father, he died by accident, and I will no longer bear the guilt of thinking I did." As soon as he uttered those words, Suresh instantly felt a surge of relief.

"All of my life," he said, "I've been kind and caring towards you, feeling sorry for your grief over my father's death, and hoping someday you would change and be a mother to me, like you once were, a long time ago. But it doesn't look like you would change. I can't live under your control anymore. I'm afraid, now you've lost me."

The unprecedented seriousness in Suresh's voice caused Manjula to immediately stop crying. She realised then he had had enough. Right there and then she knew she had indeed lost him. The love/hate relationship she had had with her stepson had finally come to an end. And for all her years of threatening and controlling him, she felt helpless in that moment. And she was now at a loss for words.

Uncle Navin then butted in, saying, "It's time to go, Manjula."

Manjula could not look at Suresh now. It was as if she suddenly realised how she had mistreated him, an innocent boy, and she remained in a taciturn mood and let Uncle Navin take her by the arm and escort her to the car, and they got in and drove away.

After Manjula and Uncle Navin left, Suresh had a bath and cooked, and after he and the dog had dinner, he sat in the hammock and played the mouth organ.

The tremendous guilt that he had been carrying over his father had dissipated, after he stood up to Manjula and defended himself, and now his heart felt light. He could lucidly see now how Manjula had manipulated and blamed him, putting him on a guilt trip, and wrongfully punished him for so many years. He now saw her in a different light, and the bona fide love he had for her was now shattered. He knew now that he could not go on living the way he was, things would have to change, but at the moment he did not know what he would do or where to turn.

He fell asleep that night contemplating his next move, and in the morning he rose early and got ready to go to work.

Rex was up to his old tricks again, hiding his sandal this time, and within spending a few minutes looking for it, he found it outside his shed buried in a pile of dirt. This set him back, and when he showed up for work he was late by just five minutes.

"You're late!" Abdul shouted at him.

He sucked his teeth.

Abdul flew into a fit of rage at this and raised his hand and threatened, "I'll box your ears for being rude!"

Suresh looked him straight in the eye, and said, "I dare you to do so."

Abdul was taken aback at the sudden change in Suresh, bravely standing up for himself. He would have boxed Suresh's ears but be backed down because he realised that he was getting too old now to come up against such a virile young man, and he slowly lowered his raised arm. "I'll dock half an hour of your pay," he then said. And he instructed Suresh to work on a dresser for a client.

Suresh worked all day on the dresser, but his mind was busy with thinking of his life and what steps he should be taking in attaining autonomy. He wrestled with his thoughts as he sawed away at the wood, sweating profusely as he did, his mind giving him one advice then changing, constantly vacillating. However, by the end of the day, he made up his mind and knew exactly what he should be doing with his present situation with Abdul.

When he was ready to leave, Abdul stood by the door entrance and, like he would usually do, he counted his pay for the day and handed it to him, "Here's your pay for the day," he said, and added, "I've deducted half an hour's worth for being late."

"But I was only late by five minutes," Suresh spoke up.

"I've done this before, now what are you going to do about it?"

Suresh took the cash and shoved it in his trousers pocket and said, "This is the last time you're going to treat me this way, Abdul."

Abdul crinkled his brows, and asked, "What do you mean by that, man?"

Suresh dusted the sawdust off his clothes and he grabbed his lunch container and headed out the door, with Abdul following, then, turning to look at Abdul again directly in the eye, answered slowly and deliberately, "What I mean by that is I wouldn't be coming back here no more."

Flabbergasted by the news, Abdul responded, "I need you, man. You just can't walk out on me now."

Suresh sucked his teeth and got on his bicycle. "Just watch me," he said, and he rode away.

And Abdul was left with his mouth open.

The immense misery that Abdul had caused him, that had strained Suresh's shoulders for so many years, was lifted, and Suresh slept soundly that night. He stayed home the next day and pondered what to do next. He decided he would go to the market and meet with the vendor who had sold him the bottle of perfume he had bought for Seya. The man was a newcomer to the village and knew nothing about him, and he seemed like a good person to approach for a job.

When the man saw him, he smiled and said, "You need something else for your lady friend, eh?"

Suresh had convinced himself that he was deluding himself about Seya, and that this point, he had no intention of going to see her. "I'm here to ask you a favour—"

"I'm Danny."

"Suresh. I'm out of a job and looking for some work. Do you have anything I can help you out with?"

Danny scratched his head and thought for a moment, then said, "No, man, I don't need help at the moment. Sorry, man."

Manjula's girlfriends at the market were craning their necks, trying to catch the conversation between Suresh and Danny, but they were out of reach. "I wonder what he's up to this time?" one of them asked.

"Probably checking out the price of perfume for some woman," another one said.

"Do you know of anyone who needs help?" Suresh asked Danny. "I can do carpentry, I can cut cane, work in the rice field, work in the sawmill, any kind of labour job."

Danny thought again and said, "Sorry, man, I can't think of anyone who is hiring at the moment."

Suresh caught Manjula's friends looking at him just that moment, and he thought it was just as well Danny did not have a job at the market for him, for these women would make life miserable for him. He thanked Danny, and then walked over to them, and asked, "Do you know Neighbour Bertha?"

At the mention of her name, the women became visibly shaken up; they had heard of the fire-rass.

"Neighbour Bertha is a friend of mine," was all Suresh had to say.

Terrified, one of the women said, "We are *your* friends also. Aren't we gals?" The other two women shook their heads in agreement, their eyes also wide with fear.

Suresh rode away on his bicycle, and he smiled, thinking that he had now settled the scores with the people who had tormented his life; Manjula, Abdul, and Manjula's friends at the market. And his heart now felt even lighter.

Chapter Nine

Fire By The Seashore

The next day Suresh woke up bright and early and made breakfast. Then he got the metal coffer, where he kept a few things of sentimental value and some cash, and he counted the cash. He had saved up a few good dollars, which would last him for at least three months for food and necessities. He hoped that by the end of then he would find some kind of work and make changes to his life. He decided he would take a couple of days off and go back out and look for work again. Given his reputation as one who had killed his father, it would be nearly impossible to find work in the village, but, he optimistically thought, there must be one good soul who would take pity on him and hire him.

At lunchtime he had a craving for Chinese lo mein, but in being frugal, he stayed home and picked a baigan in the garden and cooked that up with saltfish and roti. After lunch, he did not bother taking care of the yard or cleaning Manjula's house, but he stayed in the shed and took care of the little things he had long meant to do.

He was sitting at the kitchen table darning a shirt when Neighbour Bertha dropped by.

"That's a woman's job," she said straightaway, "you need a wife to do that for you."

"That's exactly what I need now, a nice wife to take care of me. But I'm now out of a job and can't afford a wife." And he went into explaining to her how he walked out on Abdul.

"You did the right thing, that man was taking advantage of you. Blasted scamp!" she said and cackled with laughter. "But that shouldn't stop you from taking a wife."

"I only have money to feed one for three months."

Giving him a benevolent smile, she said, "I will help you out until you get back on your feet."

"But I can't take money from you, Neighbour."

"Eh, eh, nonsense! You are like a son to me. And, furthermore, if you need a place to stay, you can come and live with me, you and your wife."

Suresh smiled, and said, "You are a kind woman, like a mother to me."

"I will take care of you, but under one condition, that you heed my advice and find a wife." She paused for a moment, then asked, "Have you seen the gal lately?"

"Not since Saturday," he answered. "And I'm not sure I want to see her again."

"Does this change of mind have anything to do with Manjula?"

"Manjula's mother died and she left on Sunday for the funeral, and she warned me not to see Seya. But that doesn't matter anymore. She no longer has control over me. By the way, I stood up to her and told her I did not kill my father, that it was an accident."

"That's what I've been telling you for years, but you were so hard ears you wouldn't listen to me. I'm glad you've finally come to your senses." Then right after, she said, "Then if Manjula has no control over you, why not visit the gal?"

"To tell you the truth, I don't know if Seya loves me, Neighbour Bertha. I feel like I've been fooling myself about her all along. She seemed to have been involved with a man named Mister Gareth, and I don't know if he's still around or if she still loves him. And I shouldn't get involved with a woman who loves another man."

"Definitely not, I agree. But you don't know this for sure, my son. I see romance playing on your eyelids as I speak, and I know you're in love with her. Go and see her, and find out if she loves you."

Neighbour Bertha then took the shirt Suresh was darning, and she finished darning the pocket. "Go have a bath and get ready to go. I will press the shirt and a pair of trousers for you." And she got the coal iron and pressed the clothes on the kitchen table.

Before Neighbour Bertha had the chance of coaxing him any further, Suresh was all dressed and ready to leave. And he went in the flower garden and picked a bunch of *pink jump & kiss flowers* to take to Seya. And he left Rex at home and took off.

* * *

It was a sweltering, breezeless afternoon, with the sun beating down on the seashore and turbid waves washing ever so languidly on the shoreline. The seagulls were basking in the sun and squawking as they reached down to catch fish in the sea, and four-eyed fish were riding the waves by the hundreds, jumping above the water and diving into it playfully only to surface to be a feast for the birds. The branches of the coconut trees that lined the shoreline were still today, drooping from the heat of the day.

Now that Neighbour Bertha had spurred him on to see Seya, Suresh's qualms about Seya left him, and his heart was racing with excitement and optimism as he hurried along the seashore. He took off his sandals, which were slipping and sliding in the sand, and he held them in his hands as he ran barefoot so he could get there faster, the sand hot against his feet.

He was panting for breath when he reached Seya's shack, and he found her on the seashore, dressed in a pale yellow sari, her long hair pinned up in a bun coiffure, and she was barefoot. She was picking driftwood of which she was holding a bundle, and Rexana was by her side.

When she saw him, she smiled shyly, and said, "I had a feeling you would come by today."

Suresh asked, "Did you miss me?"

She averted her head, lowered her lashes and gave a nod.

"I missed you, too," Suresh said, and thought deep down in his heart, even when he wanted to shut her out of his mind, a part of him was so longing to see her. Being in love with her addled his mind for a moment, then he quickly regained his composure and asked, "Is the wood for the mud stove?"

"I'm picking driftwood to light a fire on the seashore," she answered, and with a concerned look on her face, went on to say, "I hope you don't get into trouble for coming to see me."

"You don't have to worry about that anymore," Suresh said, and he handed her the pink jump & kiss flowers. "Here, I've picked these just for you. They're fresh and beautiful just like you."

Seya's limpid green eyes lit up with another smile, and she dropped the bundle of driftwood she was holding and took the flowers. "No man has ever brought me flowers. This is so thoughtful of you," she said and inhaled the delicate scent of the flowers.

Suresh picked a flower from the bunch and stuck it in her hair, and said, "I guess no one else has ever done this, either."

Seya shook her head, then said, "I will have to put them in water before they start wilting. Wait here, I'll be back." She left Suresh standing there and ran inside the shack and arranged the flowers in a small blue vase and left them on her coffee table and, shortly after, returned to join him on the seashore.

Gathering up the bundle of driftwood she had dropped, she said to him, "Take this bundle and place it over by the log, while I pick some more."

As she handed him the driftwood, Suresh was aware of her being so near to him, he could almost feel her warmth. He had dreamed so long of being close to her, touching her, caressing her long hair, and now she was in hand's reach. As quickly as the urge came, though, he brushed it aside and took the driftwood over to the log, and he joined her in picking some more off the shore.

"Pick the ones that are dry, for they will burn quickly," she said to him, "the damp ones would obviously not burn."

Once again, Suresh was distracted by her bending down to pick the wood, looking so beautiful and graceful, with her sheer yellow sari gently blowing in the wind, scattering her delicate scent about. And as she was doing so, she was softly singing an Indian love song, singing in that high-pitched, nasal, sing-song tone. He had never seen her so happy. And he joined her in singing the song as he went about gathering a handful of wood and adding it to the pile that she had picked.

Seya added another handful to the pile, then she squatted down on her haunches and went about sifting through the sand for small twigs to use for tinder. Once she gathered a small pile, she lit it with a matchstick, fanning it with a piece of paper until it grew into a flame.

"You handle this like an expert, you must do this often," Suresh said.

She told of her affinity with fire, saying, "I usually do this on Friday afternoons if it's not raining. I love sitting by the fire on the seashore. There's something so soothing about it."

They added the driftwood onto the heap, one piece carefully placed at a time, and soon there was a roaring fire.

"Let's sit on the log," Seya then invited, and both of them went and sat, sitting a few inches apart, and for a while they were in silence as they stared at the flames as they leaped and danced and crackled, as the waves were lapping softly against the shore. Now a slight breeze was blowing, scattering the smoke about, from which emanated a sweet wood smell that adhered to their clothes and made them feel hotter than it was, though it was a heat that was soothing, as Seya had mentioned, and conducive to a relaxed atmosphere.

Suresh then broke their silence, taking the chance of broaching the subject of her past life, and he said, "I'd like to find out more about you, Seya, tell me the real story of your life."

He had struck at an auspicious moment, for Seya was now ready to talk, and she began giving a highly affecting account of her past life, elucidating the mysteries that surrounded her. Looking out at the sea with a faraway look in her eyes, she began by candidly saying, "I once was in love with someone."

"Mister Gareth?"

"Yes," she said, ascertaining what he had suspected all along. "He was the twenty-one-year-old son of a white overseer of a sugar plantation." She paused for a brief moment, then went on to say, "I fell for his blue eyes and golden hair and his handsome face. So did all the other girls who worked at the plantation with me.

"One time, while I was out in the fields, late in the day when everyone else had gone home, Mister Gareth came strolling by." She stopped now as if hesitant to go on.

"You can tell me what happened. I wouldn't judge you, Seya," Suresh prompted her on.

"Everyone else did," she said. "If I tell you, I'm afraid you would not come by to see me again. You'll also treat me like an outcast."

"Then that would make two of us."

Seya then let her long hair down and absentmindedly began combing it through with her fingers.

"Go on, tell me the rest of the story," Suresh urged.

"Mister Gareth took me in the bushes that day and —" Too shy to say the words, she stopped.

Suresh finished the sentence for her: "He made love to you."

She nodded, and paused for a moment as though reminiscing, then she went on to say, "I had not known a man before, he was the first. My parents had chosen a husband for me but I did not love him. I thought it was my only chance of knowing what it was like to be in love with someone like Mister Gareth."

"But was he just using you, Seya, did he take advantage of you?"

"He told me he was in love with me," Seya explained. "He said he was in love with me the first time he laid eyes on me, which was about six months prior when I started working for the plantation."

"Then what happened?"

Another hesitation, then she said, "I became pregnant with that one-time affair."

"So your parents found out, and they threw you out of your home."

She nodded, her eyes now brimming with tears, and, in a tremulous voice went on to say, "On that late afternoon I spent with Mister Gareth, he told me he was going on a sea voyage and that he would be back for me. He promised he would take me far away and make me his wife. When my parents threw me out, he was not around and there was no one I could turn to. I remembered this shack by the seaside where my deceased grandfather used to live when he was a fisherman, and so I left my old village and came here, that is how I ended up here." She wiped her eyes with her sari then lapsed into momentary silence.

"What happened to your baby?"

She broke down and shook with a deluge of tears this time. "I, I mis—" Silence again.

"You miscarried the baby," Suresh finished for her, and he reached out and held her hand in commiserating with her for her loss. After a moment, he asked, "Did Mister Gareth find out about the baby, and did he return to you from the sea voyage?"

"He did not find out that I was pregnant because he never returned," she said as she cried. "I went looking for him at the plantation, but the girls were not allowed to talk to me, so I don't know what became of him. Now I'm an abandoned woman."

Suresh now fell silent for a moment, assimilating the happenings in Seya's life. He understood how, given the mentality and culture of her family and friends, they would brand her a bad woman.

"Now you would also think of me as a bad woman, like all the others do," Seya said. "And because I cried all the time I was also labelled a mad woman. Really, I thought I had lost my mind." Silence fell between them again, then unable to bear it, she said, "Say something, Suresh, tell me what you think of me now."

"I truly feel bad for you, Seya. I don't think of you as bad or mad. I knew there was a reason you cried a lot, and I thought it was of a broken heart. But that doesn't change the way I feel about you. Let me hold you, Seya."

When Seya did not resist, Suresh stood up and reached down to pull her up close to him. He embraced her warm body tightly for a long while and stroked her long hair, then, looking into her eyes, said, "I wouldn't condemn you, Seya. What happened a long time ago is not my business, neither is it worth condemning you over. You were in love and did an act out of loving someone. But tell me now, have you gotten over this Mister Gareth?"

"I started to forget him shortly after you came along that stormy evening. You are so sensitive, you only show me love, and that you care about me, and—" she stared into his black eyes now, her green eyes now burning with desire, "I have fallen in love with you, Suresh. Is it wrong to now be in love with someone else? Is it a crime or a sin? Everyone else would condemn me for this. Would you stay with me, Suresh? Take me somewhere far away and let's live together forever."

A tear fell from Suresh's eye as he held her close to him, and he thought that it was only love that Seya needed to cure her crying madness. Here was a young woman who needed his love and he needed hers more than he knew. "How can I refuse you, Seya? I'm in love with you, also." As the flames continued to roar, they kissed in the golden rays of the sun and sealed their love. And Seya cried, out of pure happiness this time.

"This is what I wanted for you, Seya," Suresh said as he wiped her tears away, "to see you cry for joy. Come sit with me, and let me comb your hair. I've been dreaming of doing this for a long time now."

They took their seats back on the log, and Suresh took a comb from his trousers pocket and combed Seya's ankle-length hair, caressing it and stroking it to the very tip. "It's so soft and plenty enough to make a bed for me to sleep on," he said to her. "And it's long enough for me to make a rope and climb my way up to heaven."

Seya then smiled and said, "That feels so good. I can live my entire life with you combing my hair like this everyday."

"Then wait for me just here. I will be back, Seya," Suresh said spontaneously, and he got up and started heading back home.

Seya replenished the wood in the fire and sat there watching the flames dance, and she waited patiently for him to return.

Chapter Ten

Breaking Free

When Suresh left Seya by the fire he skipped all the way home, high as a kite. Manjula was sitting on the steps of the front stairs when he arrived. She was dressed in a long black frock and seemed thinner, her face contorted with sorrow, her long black hair in disarray. He expected a reprimand from her right away, but she said nothing, only looked at him with an inscrutable expression.

He said nothing, either, just walked passed her and went directly to the shed, where Rex greeted him with a wagging tail and his tongue hanging out. He patted the dog on the back, and said, "Come with me, boy, we're leaving here."

It was not a difficult choice to make as to what to take along, for his possessions were meagre. He got his metal box, containing his father and mother's photographs and a few other things of sentimental value, along with the few dollars he had saved up. And he decided he would take only one set of clothes, which he placed in a cloth bag. He grabbed his mouth organ, then after taking one last look around the shed, he left with Rex.

Manjula was still sitting on the front steps, and when he walked passed her, she asked, in a rather calm voice, "Where are you going, Suresh?"

Suresh was quick to answer, "I'm going where I will find love and peace and happiness at last."

"You're leaving to go with Seya?"

"Yes," he answered frankly. "I'm in love with her."

He expected Manjula to expostulate, to get into an acrimonious rant and rage over this, but to his surprise she remained calm, and, instead, in a sad voice, said, "So you're leaving me."

"I had warned you many times that I would do so someday, and the time has now come. I've done all that I can for you, now it's time for me to go my way."

"But what about me?" Manjula said and started to cry, once again trying to play with his tender heart.

This time Suresh did not fall for it, he saw her for the manipulating woman she was, and he said, "You need time alone to deal with your grief and anger, and find your loving self, the way you used to be before Pa died."

Manjula sobbed for a moment, then she said, "I heard from Ranbir and Zara. They heard of their grandmother's passing and telephoned as soon as they could. They couldn't make it for the funeral, but they promised they will be here for the nine-night."

"I'm truly happy to hear this," Suresh said, and added, "If you change your ways, you stand a good chance of having both your children back in your life."

"That's what the children said to me," Manjula said as she continued to cry. "I haven't been a good mother, I know, but now I'm willing to do whatever it takes to have them back. But what about you, Suresh?"

"You will learn how to live without me. You can soon have your own children back."

Memories of Suresh then started flooding Manjula's mind, of all the good things he had done for her; making sure she was fed the times when she could not cook for herself, drawing her a bath when she was too depressed to do so, going to the drug store to get her medicine when she was sick. She then realised how kind and caring he had been to her, and tolerant.

"What can I do to make things right?" she asked, now sounding contrite with a glint of dejection in her eyes.

"It's now too late to do anything about that," Suresh said with certitude, "my mind's made up. Goodbye Manjula." And he clicked his fingers for Rex to follow him and they walked away from her.

Just as Suresh was exiting the gate, Abdul arrived, and he asked, "Where are you going, Suresh?"

"Where I will never have to see your face again," Suresh replied.

"But you can't—" Abdul began.

Manjula came over to the gate then, and she said, "Let him go, Abdul."

Suresh walked away that late afternoon, and as he turned to take one last look, he saw Manjula leaning on Abdul's shoulder and he could hear her crying.

Neighbour Bertha was on her verandah and had been observing the exchange between Suresh, Manjula and Abdul, and she hurried down the stairs to meet Suresh. "You're leaving, my son?"

"Yes, I am, Neighbour. I've found a wife at last."

Neighbour Bertha smiled broadly and asked, "Is she the young gal, Seya?"

Suresh nodded.

"May the good Lord guide your path and make you happy and prosperous, and may you be blessed with many children," she said. She then reached into her frock pocket and pulled out a brown money bag, and she took out a bundle of cash. "Here, take this, you will need it," she said, "and don't refuse it for it would be an insult to me."

Suresh thanked her profusely and took the money and shoved it in his trousers pocket, and Neighbour Bertha then hugged and kissed him on his face before letting him go.

Suresh finally had the courage to break free from Manjula, and it was an exhilarating feeling. He had extricated himself from her, free at last from her control and antagonism. As he was strolling along the seashore heading towards Seya's shack, he took out his mouth organ and began playing an Indian tune. A sense of euphoria seized him as he thought of Seya waiting for him. At last he could see the sparkle of hope and happiness waiting for him.

When he reached Seya's place, she was sitting on the log, just where he had left her, and he said to her "Come, my love, let's get your canoe and row away into the sunset."

Seya began to laugh, and it was the first time Suresh heard her doing so. It was a sweet, girlish laughter, of happiness and freedom. She thrust herself into his arms and cried effusively, "You're taking me away, oh Suresh, I'm so happy. I'll make you a happy man. I'll be the best woman a man can ask for. Oh Suresh, I'm so happy." And she began to cry for joy.

Suresh began crying himself, and laughing simultaneously, their emotions running congruent. And he reciprocated, "I'm happy, too, Seya, and I'll make you a happy woman, that I promise you."

Suresh then went and untied the canoe from the stilt of the shack, and he loaded his few belongings into it, then he went and helped Seya to pack a few things and loaded those also, along with some dry food. Seya brought the blue vase of the pink jump & kiss flowers Suresh had given to her earlier that day, then she got Rexana, and along with Rex, Suresh and Seya boarded the canoe and rowed off into the warm sunset.

Chapter Eleven

A New Life

The rays of the setting sun glittered like gold on the soft waves, and the warmth washed over Suresh and Seya. It was a picturesque scenery and a new beginning of life for them. As they were rowing away from the shore, they did not look back, leaving behind their dreadful life, and all the people who had condemned them.

"We'll start life afresh," Suresh said to Seya. "We'll find a place where no one knows us and build a new life. But first, I will make an honourable woman out of you and marry you, my love."

"Oh Suresh, this is really like living a dream," Seya said.

The evening itself was a dream. After the sun went down, a bright full moon and millions of stars emerged, casting a brilliant light that sparkled like diamonds on the calm coastal waters as a pleasant breeze was blowing. Suresh and Seya rowed along the coast until they came to another village, and they continued on to the next, and the next. A vast stretch of vacant land then followed, and soon they came upon a small, secluded seaside village, far enough away from where they once lived. Here, a few houses on stilts were scattered among the coconut trees, and the oil lamps were burning as the villagers were relaxing after dinner.

"We'll get off here and I'll see if I can find us shelter for the night," Suresh said, and they brought the canoe to shore.

As soon as they disembarked, Rex and Rexana took off playing.

Suresh and Seya then walked to the nearest house, which was old and small and the greenheart wood was unpainted, the stilts spindly. A kerosene oil lamp was burning within, the wavering flame casting long shadows on the verandah. Without hesitation, they headed up the stairs and knocked on the door and waited, hoping that the occupant would answer.

After what seemed like a long wait the top half of the door swung open with a creak, and they were met by a short stout old fisherman, of Amerindian descent, with dishevelled grey hair and a craggy face, wearing a faded white shirt and matching trousers. "What brings you here at this time of the evening?" he asked in a low husky voice, squinting at them with small, deep-set black eyes.

"We've come from a faraway village to set up life here," Suresh was quick to answer. "I am Suresh, and this is my betroth, Seya. Can you provide shelter for us for tonight?"

The man looked them over and said, "Strangers from another village. Why did you leave your village, children?"

"To seek a better life for ourselves," Suresh answered.

"To seek a better life for ourselves," Seya echoed.

The man was skeptical and asked, "Did you make any trouble at home?"

"No, no, nothing like that," Suresh said, and he went on to explain his and Seya's situation, divulging only that they wanted to be together but his stepmother was against it.

The old fisherman was taken by the story and quickly took pity on them, and he opened the bottom half of the door, and said, "Come, come into my humble abode, and make yourselves comfortable."

The fisherman's little one-bedroom house overlooked the sea, and the vast surrounding land belonged to him. The furniture in the sitting room consisted of a torn red sofa, a decrepit rocking chair, and a scarred centre table. The floor was bare and worn, and hanging from the walls were ropes and fishing nets, and in a corner were rods and reels, all emitting a rank sea scent. A tiny kitchen served as a dining room with no table or chairs, and in a corner was a mud stove and a counter on which were all of the utensils and spices the old man possessed.

Suresh and Seya entered the house and the old man gesticulated for them to sit on the sofa, and when they did, he took a seat in the old rocking chair.

For a moment he said nothing, just stared at them and rocked, the chair creaking as he did. Then he reached for his pipe on the centre table, and he lit it. He took a puff, then shaking his head in commiseration, said, "I fully understand your situation. I had once loved a woman when I was young like you, Suresh, she was the daughter of the Chief of my tribe, a very beautiful young girl. But, you see, the Chief had chosen another man from the tribe for her. I became enraged with jealously of him, and, one day, I laid wait for him and beat him up badly." He paused to take another puff of the pipe and blew the smoke out heavily, then continued on. "Because of that I was driven from the tribe and my home, and I came to this village, my hope of marrying dashed. I left all my customs behind and became friends with the local Indians and blacks, and I settled down as a fisherman. I never loved another. I ended up living alone for all these years. I wouldn't want this to happen to both of you. I will give you shelter for the night, but," he paused again before saying, "you will have to sleep separately until you are married. Have you had intimate relations as yet?"

"Not as yet," Suresh answered, and looked over at Seya.

"Not as yet," Seya echoed with a bashful smile.

"Good," said the old man. "You are decent people."

"We will do so once we get married," Suresh said.

"You both are of marriageable age, aren't you?"

"Yes, we are," said Suresh, "I'm twenty-one and Seya is—"

"Sixteen," Seya said demurely.

Suresh then asked, "Can you find us a priest to perform a wedding ceremony?"

"I'd be more than happy to do so for you two young people. I will even bear witness for you."

"You are so kind to us," Seya said.

"I wouldn't want what had happened to me to befall you both," said the old fisherman. "I'm a lonely man now, with no wife and no children. Maybe you can be my children from now on."

"We'll be happy to be considered your children," Suresh said, speaking for himself and Seya, knowing that they both were, in a way, parentless.

"We'll be happy to be considered your children," Seya repeated softly.

The old man then changed the subject, and asked, "How did you get here?"

"By canoe," Suresh answered.

"Have you some belongings?"

"We've brought a few things, and some dry food."

"Go and fetch your things," the old man said, "and I will prepare you a place to sleep. Have you had dinner?"

"Not as yet," Suresh answered.

"I haven't had dinner as yet, either," said the old man. "I was just preparing the ingredients to make some *pepperpot* with beef when you knocked on the door. I would like you to join me."

"How can we refuse?" Suresh said.

And Seya said, "I love pepperpot."

"I will start cooking while you're getting your belongings."

"Oh, we have two other little mouths to feed," Suresh said.

The fisherman looked at him puzzlingly, and said, "I thought the two of you did not have an intimate relationship."

"We haven't," Suresh said, "we've brought our two dogs with us."

The fisherman threw his hands up in the air and laughed, saying, "Oh, I see. Don't worry, there is food enough to feed them also."

And Suresh left with Seya to get their belongings from the canoe.

By the time they returned, the fisherman's house was filled with the aroma of *cassareep* mingled with rice and bread and the smoke from the burning wood of the mud stove.

"I have no forks and knives to eat with, I hope you're okay with eating with your fingers," he said to them.

"That's all right with us," Suresh said. "We're used to that."

The fisherman then placed three straw mats on the kitchen floor for them to sit and eat, and he dished out three enamel plateful of steaming pepperpot and served it up with rice and bread. Suresh and Seya took their seats on the floor and the old man joined them, and they ate heartily as the old man repeated the sad story of his love interest with the daughter of the Chief.

When they were finished, after bringing a basin of water to wash their hands, the old man offered them some Ovaltine, and he made it on the mud stove and poured them into enamel cups, and after pouring himself a shot of *piwari*, took his seat back down. "Do you have any plans laid out for your future?" he asked.

"We've only decided to leave our village just today," Suresh explained. "I'm a carpenter by trade and have left that all behind. I hope to find some work and set up my own carpentry shop someday."

"I will help you in whatever way I can," offered the old man benevolently. "Let's discuss this after you've had a good night's sleep and after you get married."

"How would we be able to repay you for your kindness?" Suresh asked.

"You can repay me with your company," the old man answered. "I have no relatives here, just a few good friends, but they cannot always be with me, and times could get very lonesome. So, perhaps, you can keep my company from time to time."

"That's the least we can do," Suresh said.

And Seya repeated, "That's the least we can do."

Rex and Rexana were then called to the verandah and were fed. Then the fisherman took Suresh and Seya downstairs and showed them the outdoor latrine in the backyard. "I have a small bathroom upstairs but there's no running water," he told them, "we have to fetch water from the only pipe here downstairs. Grab a bucket each." They fetched the water upstairs, and took turns to wash up.

When they were ready for bed, the old fisherman relinquished his bedroom—consisting of only a single spring bed with a coconut fibre mattress—to Seya, and he placed two cots in the sitting room for himself and Suresh to sleep on.

When Suresh laid his head on the pillow that night, while the fisherman was snoring on the cot beside him, his heart felt like pink cotton candy, sweet and light. It was the first time in his entire life that he felt that way. All the worries, pain and anger and guilt that had plagued him since he was a child were all left behind with Manjula and Abdul. He now felt like he was floating on soft white clouds. He was so happy that night that he did not sleep at all, same with Seya, she pinched herself from time to time to make sure she was not having a dream.

The sun rose at the break of dawn, bright and glorious, and Suresh and Seya got up when the old man did, and he offered to cook them breakfast.

"My woman is a good cook, and so am I," Suresh said, "maybe we can do the cooking instead."

"I'd be more than happy to do so," Seya offered.

"Let me have the pleasure of spoiling the two of you, like I would if I had my own children," the old man said affectionately in his husky voice.

He then went down the street to the market and bought some cassava and a piece of fresh pork, and he returned home and lit the mud stove and, with pride and joy, cooked up cassava bread and garlic pork served with tea.

While they were sitting on the straw mats on the kitchen floor and eating, the old man said, "The first thing you should do is to get married. I have a friend who's a Christian pastor, Pastor Nelson, who, I'm sure would be happy to marry you. We will go to him right after breakfast and you'll tie the knot. I don't want anyone to accuse me of harbouring an unwed couple at my house. This is a risqué thing that would straightaway start an adulterous scandal."

"We don't want that," Suresh said, and as soon as they were through with breakfast they headed into the village to a small church, painted white.

Pastor Nelson, an affable-natured black man in his fifties, tall and thin, greeted them with a pleasant smile, and after he heard of their story he was willing to marry them, and both Suresh and Seya tied the knot with the old fisherman bearing witness.

"I'm so happy," Seya said to Suresh, her smile evincing the excitement she was feeling.

"So am I," Suresh responded, inebriated with desire for her. "We've done the right thing."

The old fisherman said, "I will provide you with a tent for your wedding night which I will erect on my land. You can stay in the tent as long as necessary until you establish yourselves in a permanent house." And he added, "Choose anywhere on my land, and you can build a house. I will not charge you for the land." Suresh thought it was a magnanimous offer, and he reciprocated by offering the old fisherman all the money he had, his and Neighbour Bertha's put together, but the old man refused, saying, "I will help you out in whatever way I can, I promise. In a couple of days we will discuss your future in carpentry. There's nothing more I would like than to see the two of you succeed." The old man thought he could vicariously live his life through this couple, a life he had been robbed of by another.

The fisherman then got his friends, the amiable and gregarious Vijay and Chandni, a middle-aged Indian couple who had no children, and they, along with Suresh, helped to erect the tent along the seashore on the fisherman's land. Chandni rounded up some of her lady friends from the village and they decorated the tent for the wedding night, with fresh flowers and earthen lamps, and they lit incense.

While Rex and Rexana spent the night on the seashore, Suresh and Seya spent the night there in the tent under the moon and stars. They were now sitting at the entrance of the tent, looking out at the ocean glazed in moonlight.

Suresh put his arms around Seya and said, "We're so lucky," and he looked around the tent at the oil lamp burning and soft bedding spread out on the earthen ground, "this is our home now. We have a home of our own, Seya."

"I still think I'm only dreaming," said Seya.

Suresh pinched her arm and said, "No, this is real, my love."

"I will do a *puja* in the morning to celebrate our new found life."

Suresh's father had been a Hindu, but after he had passed away Manjula had never kept up with the religion, so Suresh was not particularly religious, but he said, "If that's what you want to do, then do it."

He then took his comb from his trousers pocket and said, "Let me comb your hair, Seya." And he began combing Seya's hair.

That subtle act of affection and seduction let to the passionate consummation of their marriage, to the sounds of the crashing waves and the breeze gently blowing.

The next morning Seya woke up early, and she arranged the pictures of her Hindu gods, Krishna and Rama and Hanuman—which she had brought along with her—against the inside wall of the tent, and she lit diyas and incense and did her puja while Suresh looked on.

Shortly after she was finished, the old fisherman came by to bring them breakfast, cassava bread and garlic pork again, and some freshly sliced mangoes. The newly weds spent the rest of the day being spoiled by the obsequious Vijay and Chandni and the fisherman himself, as well as Pastor Nelson who gifted them with a kerosene stove, and whose wife, the benign Claudia, brought along a bouquet of red roses. They brought mostly food and drinks, and many felicitations, and the Pastor brought them some clothes which were sent by the missionaries from abroad, which they would distribute to the needy. Suresh and Seya soaked up the love they were shown, and they took every moment they could to love and frolic in the sun and moonlight, drinking in the pleasures that life had to offer them.

* * *

The old fisherman left them to enjoy themselves for a couple of days and he went out fishing on his boat. He had retired from commercial fishing and only did so now to feed himself and share with his friends. He caught a fat catfish on the third day and brought it back to his house to cook for Suresh and Seya.

"Come and have lunch with me," he said to them at the tent, "we have business to discuss."

Right after a hot curry catfish lunch, the old fisherman got down to business. He took Suresh and Seya to his bottom-house where he had a workshop. "I used to build canoes at one time in my life," he explained to Suresh, "but it did not turn out to be so profitable, so I turned to fishing. Now I have this workshop with all the necessary tools you can use to start up a carpentry shop. Just your luck."

"Just my luck," Suresh repeated. "I can't believe it."

"I suggest you do," the fisherman said in his husky voice and smiled.

It seemed too good to be true, but it was really, and Suresh was beside himself. Things were finally taking a turn for the good in his life and it all seemed so surreal to him. He thrust himself in the fisherman's arms and picked him up and hugged him tightly, saying, "Thank

144

you, thank you so much. God has heard my years of cries."

"You can start right away," the fisherman said once he was put down on his feet, "I have a few projects for you. And I will pay you nicely."

Seya was so overjoyed that she started crying.

"First you will start with building me a new rocking chair. You have all the tools, and I have a load of greenheart wood."

Suresh did not waste any time and started right away on the rocking chair. Working on the project with ardour, he spent the rest of the afternoon on it, and by the following day he had it varnished and completed.

When he showed it to the fisherman, the fisherman took out a $10.00 bill, and said, "This is what you've earned, my boy." It was the most money Suresh had ever earned for building a piece of furniture. "Now I want you to build me a new sofa. I have some nice blue fabric you can use." That earned him another ten dollars. The next project was a bed frame, and the old fisherman took out another ten dollar bill and handed it to Suresh. Suresh had completed the three projects in a week and earned more money than he used to make on a monthly basis.

Suresh was adept in carpentry, and the fisherman was so impressed with the excellent quality of his work that he bragged about it to his friends Vijay and Chandni, and they commissioned Suresh to make a sitting room cabinet. Paster Nelson was shown his work, and he in turn commissioned Suresh to build a table and a set of chairs. And the word began to spread in the small village, and next thing you know, Suresh was taking on full time work and was making a decent income, which he saved up in dreams of building a house someday. The fisherman had offered a piece of land for free, and all he had to do was save enough money for the house.

Suresh did not aspire to gain vast wealth or anything grandiose, only something rudimentary, in fact, he only wanted a small house, with two bedrooms, a kitchen and dining room in one, a sitting room, and a verandah, which was the quintessential house in the village at the time. The fisherman had a couple of friends who would help him to build the house for a small fee. He would build his own furniture, and just what was necessary and not excessive. He chose to have a mud stove instead of a modern appliance, oil lamps instead of electricity, and he would have an outside bathroom and latrine. He had his plans all laid out, and Seya was most agreeable to them.

Seya, in the meantime, had taken up sewing from Chandni, who gave her the old Singer treadle sewing machine she had because she had long given up sewing for a living due to her failing eyesight. She managed, however, to teach Seya how to make baby clothes, and Seya was making the clothes and supplying them to stores, which brought in a steady income for her. With two steady incomes, and not having to pay rent for the tent the old fisherman had provided to them—a real boon to their lives—Suresh and Seya were able to save up money for their little dream house in a year's time.

On a sweltering Saturday afternoon, while it was raining heavily, Seya was cooking on the kerosene stove in their cozy little tent. She was making roti and curried chicken. Suresh was sitting on the ground at the entrance of the tent chewing on sticks of sugarcane and drinking coconut water from a green coconut, and he was absent-mindedly looking out at the rain and glancing over at her.

It then just dawned on him that there was something different about Seya for the past few weeks. Her dark skin seemed to glow with all the happiness life was bringing to them both, but there was something else he could sense. And it was when she was in a side profile position while she was cooking that he noticed the little bump in her belly. And his heart instantly leaped for joy.

He got up and went and stood behind her and put his arms around her belly, and he said, "You know you're carrying my child."

She laughed, and said, "I was waiting for you to notice."

"I will have our house built in time for our firstborn," Suresh promised, beaming from ear to ear, and he turned her around and hugged and kissed her.

The very next day, he went out and got the wood for the house, and he selected a piece of the fisherman's land, facing the sea, and with the help of the fisherman's friends, building commenced. After the constant hammering of nails and sawing of wood and rustling of zinc, the time came when the house was finished, just a month before Seya was to give birth. That gave Suresh enough time to build a sofa, cabinet, and centre table for the sitting room, and a bed frame, which he furnished with a sponge mattress. He deliberated whether he should paint the house and decided to leave it unpainted, and Seya thought it was a good idea because she loved the sweet scent of the greenheart wood and the rawness of it. With the house all completed, they moved into it.

During the time spent there in their new village, Suresh and Seya made friends with the locals, who embraced them with bona fide affection and made them part of the community of friends, lending them certain cachet. Now Suresh and Seya had the life they so deserved, and the respect, which they cherished. And life became what it was meant to be; a life of love, peace, and happiness.

On a hot and sunny afternoon, while Rex and Rexana were attending to their recent litter of six pups as Suresh and Seya were sitting out on their verandah relaxing, their friends, the fisherman and Vijay and Chandni came calling.

Suresh was just then sitting on a chair, combing Seya's long hair, when he noticed them and ran downstairs to greet them.

He hugged and kissed them, and said, "Come, join us."

"How's my daughter Seya doing today?" asked the fisherman.

"She was having labour pains earlier today," Suresh answered.

Just then they heard Seya groaning, and they rushed up to the verandah and found that her water had broken.

"Quick!" Chandni said, "Help me to carry her to the bedroom and I'll help in delivering the baby."

Suresh did so, and then waited out on the verandah with the fisherman and Vijay. After hearing Seya moan and groan for a while, a happy laughter escaped Chandni's lips, and she said, "Come, Suresh, and see your baby."

"It's a boy!" Suresh exclaimed when he held the tiny bundle. "I think I'll name him Raheem, after my father. Let's get the villagers and celebrate!"

That same afternoon, Chandni made sweets and the villagers came and celebrated the birth of Suresh and Seya's baby. Later in the evening, when everyone was gone, Suresh sat out on the verandah and played an Indian tune on the mouth organ, with Rex and Rexana and their litter of six pups beside him. And Suresh said to himself, "Six children is what I want from Seya also."

And Suresh played the night away.

A few weeks after Raheem was born Pastor Nelson had a talk with Suresh, saying, "It is time that we christen or baptise the child."   And he went into explaining the process to Suresh.

"Baptise my child?" Seya said to Suresh. "What does that mean?"

"Christians christen a baby to name the child and for claiming the child for Christ through the sprinkling of water on the child's head."

"But I am not Christian," Seya protested. This would then spark arguments between them that persisted throughout Seya's child-bearing years. Pastor Nelson managed, however, to persuade her, and the child was christened and was given a Christian name, Joseph, and his Indian name remained Raheem.

With the commitment made, Suresh started taking the child to church on Sundays, and Seya would stay at home and do her puja or sometimes she and Chandni would visit a Hindu temple in the village.

Seya was large with her second child when, as she was having lunch with Suresh one day at their carpentry workshop which Suresh had set up at their bottom-house, she said, "My second child will have Hindu rites performed when he is born."

"We cannot have our children divided by religion," said Suresh adamantly.

Again, Paster Nelson intervened when the second child was born, and the child was baptised and given a Christian name, David, but was called Arjun. The same thing happened when the third child was born, and his Christian name was Peter and his Indian name Akshay. Likewise for the fourth child, Mark was Balvan, and the fifth child, James was Ishwar.

By this time, Seya's body was getting tired and worn from having babies, and she said to Suresh, "Ishwar is my last child."

"But you still haven't produced a daughter as yet," Suresh said.

"No more babies," Seya insisted.

Suresh kissed her on the head and attempted to inveigle her by saying, "Just one more try, my love. I will buy you a nice gold chain for trying."

Seya resisted Suresh's amorous advances for a few weeks, then on a bright moonlit night while she and Suresh were laying in bed in their little house by the seaside, she reconsidered things, not because of the gold chain Suresh had promised her or the warmth of his skin next to hers, but she had always dreamed of having a girl baby. And on that auspicious night, she whispered in his ear, "I will bear you one more child, but under one condition."

"And what is that?"

"That this child is given Hindu rites."

Suresh did not protest. He had had his way with his five boys, thanks to Pastor Nelson's influence, but he now could not overlook his wife's wish.

The sixth child came, and in answer to the couple's prayers, it was a girl baby. And they named her Sushila. And what a pretty, dark skin, curly hair baby she was. Seya was given her gold chain as Suresh had promised, and she had her way and did her pujas with the baby while Suresh took the five boys to Sunday school at the church. But it was not before long that Seya, under the influence of Pastor Nelson's wife, Claudia, started sending the girl baby with the boys to Sunday school. However, she kept up her pujas with Sushila. And the arguments between Suresh and Seya dissolved over this matter.

Their next contention came over the education of the children.

"It's costing too much to send Raheem and Arjun to private school," Suresh said to Seya. "It's a waste of money. I am training Raheem to become a carpenter like me, and Arjun wants to be a fisherman like his Grandpa fisherman."

"If I have to starve I will see to it that all of my children have an education," Seya protested.

"What's a piece of paper worth when they're not going to use it, eh? I will train all my five boys in carpentry and we will save a lot of money."

"My children will have an education regardless if you train them to do carpentry. Once they have an education then it is up to them when they grow up to make a choice as to what profession they want to get into."

"Okay, Okay," Suresh acquiesced, "have it your way."

"And when Sushila grows up, I will send her away to England to further her education in nursing."

"Okay, have it your way," Suresh repeated.

"You will not regret this in the long run," Seya promised.

Their next disagreement came when, one day, Raheem was bullying Arjun and he took from him a toy fish that the old fisherman had given to Arjun. Arjun began bawling and ran to his mother and complained, "Ma, Raheem took away my fish."

They were at the bottom-house now, and Seya, fed up and exasperated with Raheem constantly bullying and badgering Arjun, did an unprecedented thing. She said to Raheem to go and pick her a stick from a tamarind tree in the backyard, and when Raheem brought it to her, she brandished the whip and shouted at him, saying, "I will beat you for being a bully to your brother!" And she was just about to flog Raheem.

Suresh was in his workshop and heard Seya, and he rushed out and yelled at her, saying, "Don't you dare hit the child with that stick!"

"He needs a good licking!" Seya yelled back.

"I wouldn't let you do that to my child!" Suresh expostulated.

"But everybody beats their children around here."

"Well, we're not everybody. I've never laid a finger on you since I married you, and I wouldn't stand back and watch you beat our child and condone this barbaric act." And with vehemence, he added, "No beating, that is the rule of my house!"

Seya backed down and sucked her teeth and swelled her mouth, and she stamped her feet as she walked away, never to attempt such a thing again. Suresh then reprimanded Raheem with a verbal warning, threatening he would withhold his treats if he bullied Arjun again.

The subject soon changed to something they both agreed on.

"We need to extend the house and build two more bedrooms," Suresh said. "The boys are growing and need more space."

"And Sushila should have her own room," Seya said.

"Raheem should have his own bed, and Arjun and Akshay can share a bunk bed, the three of them can be in one room. Balvan and Ishwar can share a bunk bed in one room. And Sushila will have her own room."

That was settled, and it was agreed upon that would be the project for the next year once they saved up some more money. And life went on as usual for the meanwhile.

That same year, during the adjournment of school one sunny August afternoon, Suresh got his rifle and took Raheem and they went hunting for shorebirds to curry for dinner. He caught about a dozen of them and brought them home. This was a source of excitement among the children, and they watched as Suresh sat on the kitchen floor and removed the feathers and chopped and cleaned the birds.

While he went about currying the meat for dinner on the mud stove, Seya took the five boys downstairs by the pipe by the concrete slab at the bottom of the back stairs and she bathed them, and she took them upstairs and dressed them in their home clothes. She then brought a basin of water in the sitting room and bathed baby Sushila, who was now crawling at ten months, then she rubbed her down with coconut oil and exercised her little arms and legs and powdered her, and she dressed her in a white shimmy. She then went and spread bedding on the floor of one of the two bedrooms, preparing the place for bed time, for soon after dinner, Suresh would dress the children in their night clothes and put them to bed. Sushila would sleep with her and Suresh in a crib in their bedroom. She then went and had a bath and put on a favourite sari that Suresh liked; a green one that matched her limpid sea-green eyes.

When she returned to the kitchen she lit the kerosene oil lamp for it was beginning to get dark outside, and she hung it up on the chain dangling from the ceiling. Suresh first dished out an enamel plate of hot curry and rice for Seya to feed baby Sushila and herself, and Seya took her seat on a peerah on the kitchen floor, and while she was feeding Sushila and herself, she watched as Suresh started the time-consuming process of getting things ready to feed the five boys, which he would ritually do at every dinner.

In a large round white basin, he carefully dished out the steaming rice and heaped the hot curry onto it, then he placed a scoop of mango achar on the side with six fresh *wiri wiri* hot peppers, one for him and each of the boys. He then placed the basin in the middle of the tiny kitchen floor, right in front of the mud stove, and he arranged the boys around it, giving them each a cup of water, as well as himself, and he sat down himself. As the embers in the mud stove were smouldering, Seya watched as Suresh took his time in deboning the meat with his fingers, the play of the flame of the lamp dancing about his face. Then he took his time in mixing the rice and curry with his fingers, making it tepid and finally ready to eat.

By now Seya was finished with feeding Sushila and herself. She would normally stay around and watch Suresh feed the boys, as well as himself, for it brought Suresh great pleasure to do so, but tonight she was too enervated. "I've been on my feet all day taking care of the children and the house chores and I'm tired now," she said to Suresh, "I think I'll stretch out in the hammock on the verandah and relax for a while."

"Okay, gal, after I'm finished here I'll put the children to bed and have a bath, then I'll come out and join you."

Seya tried taking Sushila along with her, but the baby starting making a fuss to stay with Suresh and her brothers, so Seya left her crawling around on the floor near to Suresh, hoping to be fed some more for she had a voracious appetite for a baby.

"Open your mouth wide," Suresh said to her, and she did so for another morsel of food, and was clapping her little mouth.

Seya washed her hands and left Suresh to go about feeding the children, and she went out on the verandah. She brought a mosquito coil and lit it and placed it nearby, and then she stretched out in the hammock.

A rainstorm began pelting the coast then, coming down in torrents, and the waves were crashing wildly, the tide high. The sitting room window was open, and the piquant scent of the curry breezed through, mingling with the incense-scented mosquito coil. Seya closed her eyes and she could hear Suresh and the children talking, while Sushila was cooing.

Suresh was asking Raheem, "What do you want to be when you grow up, Raheem?"

"A carpenter like you, Papa," Raheem answered.

And Arjun said, "I want to be a fisherman, like Grandpa fisherman." Then he suddenly exclaimed, "Ouch! Raheem just pinched me on my arm, Pa!"

"Raheem, if you pinch Arjun again, I will not let you go to Sunday school this Sunday," Suresh said, admonishing him rather sternly. "Now open your mouth, Ishwar," Seya could hear Suresh say as he was giving Ishwar a morsel of food. "Chew it well before you swallow it."

"Pa you know how to cook sweet," Balvan said.

"Papa, you didn't ask me what I want to be when I grow up . . ." the sound of Akshay's voice trailed off.

The voices slowly faded in Seya's ears, and she found herself drifting off to the sound of the rainstorm. Suddenly, she could see him, Mister Gareth, caught in the storm. The ship that carried him rode the high waves and crashed down into their folds. He clung to the railing and tried to maintain his balance, but an enormous wave washed over the deck, wrenching him away. As the sea engulfed him, she heard him calling her name with his last breath.

She had never seen the actual newspaper article of his drowning. And for all those years she had thought that Mister Gareth had abandoned her.

Suresh finished feeding the children, and he put on the boys pyjamas and kissed them all and put them to sleep in their bedroom after they had said their nightly prayers, and he lulled Sushila and put her down in her crib in his bedroom. After having a bath, he got dressed in his pyjamas as well and went out on the verandah to join Seya.

He looked down at Seya and found her asleep in the hammock. She was only twenty-six now and had gained weight with the bearing of their six children, and she looked round and healthy, and appeared so peaceful. He had brought the comb to comb her hair, which she still kept long, but he decided not to wake her. Carefully, he lifted her in his arms and took her to their bedroom and laid her down on the bed.

As the rain was pattering on the corrugated zinc roof, he cuddled up behind her, and could hear her lightly breathing, as was Sushila, and he drifted off to sleep with a satisfied mind, thinking of how blessed he was, and thinking if only Neighbour Bertha could see him now.

The End